CHAPTER 1
SKY AND STARS

Ruby slipped out of the door onto the small balcony of her flat. Sitting with her back against the wall, she stared out across the rooftops and chewed the end of her pencil.

Dear Dad

I hope you are fine. Here at home things are all good. Leo is growing fast and Mum is well. It's my birthday soon if you haven't remembered. But I expect you have. I am going to be 11, but of course you know that too! I think this year you may be planning the biggest surprise EVER. Can't wait to see what it is!

Love Ruby

XOXO

She searched the sky until she found her special star—the one that she and Dad used to wish on. She squeezed her eyes shut and wished that Dad really could read this letter and that she really would get a surprise. She held the letter to the sky, then folded the paper and put it in a brown envelope. She wrote 'Dad' in big letters and drew a star where the stamp should go. She lifted the lid off her box and looked at the photo she'd stuck inside. It was a picture of Dad with a skateboard under his arm and a trophy in his hand. He'd always told Ruby that one day she'd become a champion skateboarder, just like him, and he'd promised, PROMISED, to give her a skateboard when she was older. She'd hoped to get one for her birthday last year, but NO. So maybe this year would be it. She certainly hoped so. She put her letter in the box with all her other letters and replaced the lid. She wasn't exactly sure where Dad was, but he must be somewhere out there.

ME AND MISTER P

RUBY'S STAR

WRITTEN BY
MARIA FARRER

ILLUSTRATED BY
DANIEL RIELEY

OXFORD
UNIVERSITY PRESS

CHAPTER 2
AIR AND WATER

Saturday was going to be hot—

28 degrees hot

the weather lady on the telly said. Hotter than
Greece, she said, but Ruby knew nothing about
Greece so that didn't mean much. She kicked
off her blanket.

She could hear her brother grizzling in his
cot beside Mum's bed. A police car screamed
past on the street way below, the sound of the
sirens rolling up the grey walls of her tower
block. Ruby wasn't ready to wake up, but she

forced her eyes open. She wondered if she'd ever get a lie-in again.

Mum appeared at the door, her face pale and her eyes downcast. 'Sorry Ruby,' she said in a voice barely above a whisper, 'I didn't get a wink of sleep. Could you look after Leo for a while. I just need to try and catch up.' When Mum was like this it was hard for Ruby to know what to do. It was as if all the light had gone out of Mum's eyes and it made Ruby sad.

Mum handed Leo to Ruby and Ruby sat him on her bed. She picked up his favourite fluffy duck and made quacking sounds as she bobbed

it backwards and forwards. Mum hadn't been great for a few weeks now and when Mum was like this it meant Ruby had to step in and take her place. She didn't mind helping out with her little brother, but sometimes it was tough trying to look after Leo and Mum at the same time.

'Quack,' she said, wiggling the duck in front of Leo. She'd been trying to teach Leo to say quack for days—without any success at all. 'Quack, quack.'

Leo had lost interest in the duck and wanted his breakfast. Ruby sighed, hauled herself off the bed, pulled on some shorts and a T-shirt, and took Leo through to the kitchen. She gave him some food and then carried him to the window where something caught her eye . . . something in the sky. They went over to the window to get a better look.

She pointed up and laughed with excitement. 'Look, Leo! Up there.' She'd never seen anything like it before—not in real life, not here in the city. Floating high above the rooftops was a

colourful hot-air balloon.

Ruby screwed up her eyes to try to see better.
She watched it drift across the cloudless blue
and wondered who was in it. She imagined
herself up there looking down on the world
below and for a moment she felt as free as a bird.
'Come on,' she said, giving Leo a squeeze, 'Let's
go out. I'm sick of being caged up in here.'

She dressed Leo, checked in on Mum, who was fast asleep, then took the lift to the ground floor and set off towards the park. The High Street was always busy at this time of day. Crowded pavements and exhaust fumes added to the heat. She crossed the road and took the path which led around the outside of the park. This meant she'd go past the new skatepark, which was her favourite place in the whole world. She kept close to the graffiti wall, with all its patterns and colour, so she could blend into the background and no one would notice her. Before long she heard the rumble and clatter of wheels on concrete and out of the corner of her eye she caught flashes of colour as the skateboarders hurtled backwards and forwards, jumping, sliding, whooping, and laughing.

Everyone seemed to be having a good time. Ruby slowed her steps, but didn't stop. She recognized one of the boys from her year at school so she quickly put her head down and

hurried on. Being seen pushing your baby
brother around was definitely not cool.

She headed down the hill towards the pond.
The sunshine had brought lots of families into
the park and it made Ruby feel even more alone.

As they neared the water, Leo stuck out
his hand and said 'ACK'. Ruby laughed and
crouched down beside his pushchair.

'You did it, Leo. You said "Quack." High
five!' She lifted his little hand and bumped it
against her own and he laughed. 'Ack, ack,
ack,' he said over and over, rocking himself
backwards and forwards in his seat.

Ruby pulled a crust of stale bread out of a bag. A raft of ducks raced towards the crumbs, stabbing the water with their beaks, and swimming to and fro as they waited for more. Then suddenly everything went still and silent. Ruby frowned. A huge shadow was creeping across the pond, turning the water dark. The ducks took off in a fearful flap of feathers, squawking as they went.

Ruby looked up and gasped. Floating towards the pond was the hot-air balloon, but this time it wasn't high in the sky at all, it was barely above the trees. Close-up it was massive and she could clearly see the basket. She shielded her eyes from the sun and wondered if the light as playing tricks on her. It looked as though there was something huge and white and furry in the basket.

Leo started to cry. Ruby rubbed her eyes and looked again. She must be imagining things.

The balloon was getting lower and lower. A loud **roar** came from the burner as a burst of flame shot upwards. The balloon slowed and dropped gently towards the ground. *It's going to land,* thought Ruby, *In the park!* Ruby crouched down, as the basket of the balloon skimmed overhead, almost knocking her head off.

'Watch what you're doing,' she shouted,

trying to protect Leo and shaking her fist at the occupant of the balloon.

Now everyone in the park was looking. Shouts of panic rang in Ruby's ears as people tried to clear out of the way. With a bump and a bounce, the basket touched down on the grass and fell on its side, the giant canopy of the balloon collapsing in folds around it. Then there was SILENCE.

Everyone stood and waited.

There was some rustling and then a roar, this time *not* from the balloon.

People gasped. What was *in* there?

Something underneath the material of the balloon moved. It started as a shiver and shake, then a large lump lifted the material closest to the basket and slid slowly in Ruby's direction. Everyone else took a step back, but Ruby stood her ground. Right in front of where she was standing, the lump stopped. Five long black claws emerged, followed by a huge white paw.

Then a second paw. And then a long, furry snout and finally an entire polar bear.

Ruby was too shocked to move.

The bear retrieved a tattered brown suitcase from under the material, then stood up on its hind legs and sniffed the air. Kids and grown-ups stumbled and ran and screamed. Ruby looked up at the animal and put her hands on her hips. She knew it couldn't be a real polar bear because:

(a) polar bears don't live in these parts

(b) polar bears do not fly around in hot-air balloons

(c) polar bears do not carry suitcases

Ruby decided this must be some stupid joke and she wasn't falling for it. She glanced at the suitcase and noticed the label.

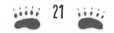

Mister P

it said in frosty blue writing. She looked at the bear again. 'Are you Mister P?' she asked.

The bear took a step forwards and, before she'd had a chance to move, it had pushed its wet, black nose right into her face.

BACKWARDS AND FORWARDS

Ruby arched her back, pulling her own nose as far away as possible from the bear's. She had to admit, joke or no joke, the breath coming out of that mouth was pretty fishy.

Leo squealed and pointed at the bear. 'Ack, ack,' he repeated over and over.

'Shut up, Leo,' said Ruby, not taking her eyes off the bear for a single moment. In truth, Ruby wasn't feeling quite as confident as she looked and there was something rather unsettling about the way the bear was staring at her. She tipped Leo's pushchair onto its back wheels and spun it around. 'Come on, Leo, time for us to get out of here.'

Ruby was certain this must be some kind of set-up. There was probably a hidden TV camera filming it all and she didn't want to be the one looking stupid. She reached the edge of the park and glanced back over her shoulder to check what was happening. To her surprise, the animal wasn't far behind her and seemed to be following in her direction. It really did look very real. She hurried on, walking quite a bit faster, heading straight for the main road. Luckily the traffic lights turned red just as she reached the crossing and the traffic came to a stop. Ruby jogged quickly across the four lanes of cars and stepped onto the pavement on the far side. This time when she looked back, the bear had just arrived at the same crossing point, but the lights were turning from red to green and the traffic was beginning to move. Ruby smiled. Now she'd get rid of him.

PEEP   PEEP   PEEEEEEEEEEEEP

Horns blared, brakes screeched, and there was a metallic THUNK as one car ran into the back of another. Ruby clapped her hand over her mouth and watched in horror. What was the crazy animal doing? Didn't he realize you couldn't just wander across a busy main road? As she continued to stare, the bear leaped and jumped around, trying to dodge oncoming cars. Finally, as a double-decker bus thundered towards him, the bear lay down flat on its

stomach with the suitcase covering his head.
Ruby hid Leo's eyes with her hand as the bus
skidded to a stop, JUST in time. The bear stayed
absolutely still.

Ruby cupped her hands and shouted at the
bear, 'Get back off the road. You have to wait
for the lights! Go on! Get BACK!' But the
bear seemed too shocked to move.

Finally, the lights went red again and Ruby
watched as a very confused bear staggered across
the road, dragging his suitcase with him. She

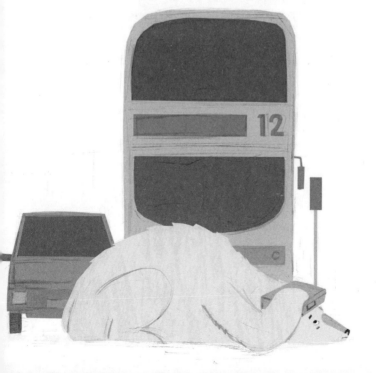

couldn't help thinking that the bear looked a bit like she felt—totally stunned!

She set off again, pushing Leo as quickly as she could. As she marched along the street, everyone stood aside to let her through. This was weird! And she didn't much like the way they were looking at her either. Then a strange, tingling feeling started in her neck. Was it her they were looking at or something CLOSE BEHIND her . . .

She stopped, took a deep breath, and turned around. The bear jumped back and widened its black eyes. It must have been RIGHT on her heels. Up close for the second time, she had to admit that it really was very large and very scary. She frowned and wondered why nobody was bothering to stop and help her—they just walked in a wide arc around Ruby as if they couldn't see the bear at all. There was only one thing for it . . . she'd have to deal with him by herself.

'Look, I don't know what you want,' she said in her sternest voice, 'but I have to tell you, you are beginning to freak me out. Now stop following me and go back to where you belong.' She pointed roughly in the direction of where she thought the Arctic might be.

The bear shook himself, but didn't move.

'Or, if it's the zoo you're after, you'd better go and ask Mr Jay in the corner shop for directions. He knows all about that kind of thing. You'll find him very helpful. Go on, off you go. SHOVE OFF!'

The bear wrinkled his nose, but showed no sign of shoving off.

Ruby shrugged. 'Look, I'm sorry, but whatever it is you're here for, I can't help you. It's been interesting meeting you, but I need to get home.'

This time Ruby walked her very fastest. The sound of polar bear paws

thud, thud, thudding,

on the pavement behind her was unmistakable. If this really was a joke, it wasn't funny any more. The closer she got to home, the more uneasy Ruby became. She made the final turn into the Hazeldown Farm Estate and broke into a run, racing towards her block of flats as fast as she could. She got through the main door and pressed the button for the lift over and over. 'Come on, come on!' she shouted at the metal doors. She wondered about using the stairs, but there was no way she could carry Leo and the pushchair up 22 flights.

Finally the ground floor light lit up and the lift door whooshed open, just as Ruby saw the bear pushing his way in through the main entrance. She dragged the pushchair into the lift and pressed the button for Floor 22. With a split second to spare, the door slid closed, putting a strong metal barrier between herself and the animal.

Ruby leaned against the wall and breathed a sigh of relief. The lift cranked into action and clunked its way up 22 floors where it ground to a stop. Ruby hoped Mum would be feeling better after her sleep. She wasn't sure whether or not to tell her anything about the bear. Perhaps it was better to keep it to herself. She didn't want to worry Mum unnecessarily.

The lift doors slid open. Ruby got her key ready, looked towards her door, and FROZE.

CHAPTER 4

IN AND OUT

The bear was right outside her flat, collapsed against her door, puffing and panting! He must have run up the stairs very quickly. Ruby wasn't sure what to do. In her opinion this was now turning into a major situation. When a polar bear is blocking the door to your home, you can't ignore it.

'Listen to me,' she said pointing her finger at the end of the bear's nose. 'Bears are not allowed in here. You are trespassing on council property. If anyone finds out you will be in BIG trouble.'

Mister P stared at the label on his suitcase.

'It doesn't matter who you are, Mister P. No

bears. None at all. Now, if you wouldn't mind, I need to get in.' Ruby tried to barge past the bear, kicking his suitcase out of the way. As the case fell on its side, the label flipped over.

Ruby's mouth went dry as she took hold of the label and read it.

The writing was as clear as day. Now Ruby realized why the bear was here. He must have got confused with her address. She crouched down and pointed at the writing on the label.

'You've come to the wrong place, mister. This is the Hazeldown Farm *Estate*. You're looking for a *farm* farm. You know, with fields and cows and sheep and stuff.'

The bear looked all around him and stood his suitcase back up, but he still didn't budge.

'OK, suit yourself. Sit here if you want, but someone will soon have you taken away. To be honest, I'd leave now, if I were you, before you're caught. You never know what they might do with you then.'

Ruby gave Mister P a hard shove and he shuffled along just enough to let her get to the door. She wasted no time in getting the key in the lock and pulling Leo into the safety of the flat. She kicked the door closed behind her, but instead of the loud slam she was expecting, the door made a soft thud and bounced back open. Wedged in the gap was one enormous hairy paw.

Now Ruby had a fight on her hands. She **pushed** the paw as hard as she could, trying to move it out of the way, but the bear **pushed** back. Ruby was nowhere near strong enough and her feet started to slide slowly across the slippery floor as the bear applied more pressure. There was nothing she could do. Before long, the bear had managed to get his huge head into her flat and after that it wasn't long before the rest of him arrived too.

Crikey! Ruby pushed her fists against her cheeks and tried not to panic. Mum hated *anyone* coming to visit and Ruby had no idea how she'd explain the arrival of a polar bear. As far as she could see, there was no way of removing him, or even hiding him. The flat was tiny—with barely enough room for the three humans, let alone a bear.

Mister P looked around and put down his suitcase. He walked straight to the living room, found a spot near the window, curled his legs underneath him, and lay down.

'Ruby?' Mum called from the bedroom. 'Ruby—is that you back?'

'Hi Mum.' Ruby tried to sound normal.

'What time is it?'

'Time to find a new flat, I think. This one is getting a bit crowded.'

'Sorry?' said Mum.

'Don't worry. Nothing. You stay in bed.'

Ruby took off her cap and ran her fingers through her hair as she searched around for some quick solution to this problem. She concluded, very fast, that there was no solution, quick or otherwise, to the unexpected arrival of a polar bear. She'd just have to get on with things as best she could and hope no one noticed. Fat chance!

Leo started crying and struggling to escape from his pushchair.

'Shhh, shhh, shhh,' said Ruby, unclipping the straps. 'We don't want Mum coming through just yet.'

It was too late. Mum was already shuffling out of her room, yawning and shielding her eyes from the glaring sunlight. She got as far as the chair near the window and sank down into it.

'Mum-um-um-um,' babbled Leo.

Mum held out her arms and Ruby handed Leo to her. He stood balancing on Mum's knee, bouncing up and down. Mum smiled and then noticed the huge furry mound. She shut her eyes tight and opened them again. 'What is that?!' she said, her voice all high-pitched and trembly.

'What?' said Ruby, because she couldn't think of anything else to say.

'THAT!' said Mum, pointing at Mister P.

'Ah, ummmmm, yes.' Ruby bit her lip. 'Well

I am not one hundred per cent sure, but I think
it's a polar bear.'

There, she'd said it. She watched the
confusion on Mum's face.

'I know you reckon I'm a bit soft in the head,
Rubes, but REALLY? A polar bear. I'm not
falling for that one.'

At that moment Mister P lifted his head and
gave a huge yawn, showing all his teeth.

Mum shrieked, leapt to her feet, and pulled
Ruby close.

'I tried to tell you,' said Ruby, gently, as she
prized herself away from Mum's vice-like grip.

'You need to stay calm. It's OK. I've got this.'

Mum's breathing was too fast, too noisy, too shallow, and she'd turned very pale. Mum's anxiety was a serious problem and, above all, Ruby needed to try to keep her calm.

'He seems very friendly,' said Ruby reassuringly. 'He won't hurt us, I'm sure.' Ruby tried hard to sound convincing.

Mum was bunching into a smaller and smaller ball in her chair and Leo was getting distressed. 'But what is a polar bear doing here . . . in our flat?'

Ruby wished she knew the answer. He certainly wasn't making life any easier.

'His hot-air balloon landed in the park and he followed me home. That's all I know.' Even as the words left her mouth, Ruby realized how completely ridiculous she must sound, but she carried on anyway. 'His name is Mister P and it says on his suitcase that he's headed for Hazeldown Farm.'

'SUITCASE?' Mum shrieked. 'HAZELDOWN?'

Mister P leapt to his feet and raised his claws. Mum struggled out of her chair and backed towards the wall.

'Get him OUT of here,'

she shouted. Mum's breath was rasping and raw, matched only by the deep growl coming from somewhere in the back of Mister P's throat.

'OK,' Ruby said firmly, putting herself between the bear and Mum. 'We all need to take a few deep breaths—me included.' Ruby demonstrated and watched as Mum and Mister P slowly followed her lead. 'In for five and out for five. In for five and out for five.' She raised and lowered her arms on each in-breath and out-breath. It was what her head teacher did when he'd decided to teach them all meditation in assembly. She kept going until Mum and Mister P seemed more under control.

'That's better,' said Ruby.

'But what are we going to do?' said Mum, her voice still shaky. 'We can't let him stay. I mean, what if someone finds out he's here and then we get thrown out and have nowhere to live? How do we feed him? How do you look after a polar bear?' Mum's breathing got fast again and then she started to cry.

Ruby took Leo from Mum. 'Perhaps you'd feel better if you went back to bed for a little while to get over the shock. I'm sure we can work things out. It may not be as bad as we think.'

'It'll probably be a lot worse than we think,' said Mum as Ruby helped her back to her room and settled Leo in his cot for a nap.

She was worried Mum might be right. How was she supposed to know how to look after a polar bear when she could barely look after her own family? One thing was for sure, when Ruby had wished for a big birthday surprise, Mister P was not what she'd had in mind.

CHAPTER 5
UP AND DOWN

The shock of the polar bear seemed to tip Mum into the darkest of places and there wasn't much Ruby could do. She took Mum a drink and sat with her, but Mum didn't want to leave her bed or her room.

Ruby scanned the fridge for something to tempt Mum's appetite. An old piece of cheese that had gone hard at the edges and some beans with green fluffy stuff growing on the top. She checked the date on the milk, took off the lid, sniffed it, and poured it down the sink. The fridge wasn't working properly in this heat.

There was nothing for it. Ruby needed a trip to the supermarket or they'd all go hungry. She found Mum's purse and emptied the contents onto the side. £35.63. That should be plenty. What was she going to do with the bear though? She didn't think she should leave him in the flat with Mum, so she supposed he would have to come with her.

Ruby stuffed the money in her pocket and got Leo ready. As she left the flat, Mister P was right behind her, like a large shadow. She pushed the button to call the lift then pointed Mister P towards the stairs. 'I'll wait for you down at the entrance,' she said as the lift door pinged open.

Mister P watched Ruby and Leo walk into the lift then tried to push his way in behind them, squashing them into the tiniest space in the corner.

'Oh for goodness sake,' Ruby muttered as she swept polar bear fur away from her eyes and mouth and tried to clear a space for Leo.

'There's no room for you in here. Polar bears use the stairs.'

It was too late, the lift doors were already closing and Mister P **roared** a roar that blasted Ruby's eardrums and shook the whole lift! The doors opened again, automatically, and Mister P gave a whimper, looking nervously behind him. Ruby couldn't see past all that fur, but she guessed that his stubby tail must have got caught.

'I told you you wouldn't fit,' said Ruby. 'Are you going to get out?'

Mister P was not going to get out. Instead he pushed himself further in.

'Well, keep your bum out the way this time.'

Ruby felt for the ground floor button and the doors closed. The lift clunked like crazy as it started its descent. Ruby wasn't sure how many kilos a bear weighed and whether the rusty lift machinery would cope. Down and down they went. Mister P's dark eyes blinked each time the

light went down another floor. They crunched
to a stop at ground level and there was a moment
of silence as the doors opened.

'Time to get out,' said Ruby. But Mister P
had other ideas. He stuck out one claw and
pressed the top button.

'What are you doing?' cried Ruby as the lift
started to go up again. 'This isn't a game you
know.'

Up and up they went and Mister P grinned
and wriggled.

When they reached floor 25, Ruby pressed
GROUND FLOOR again.

Down they went, and back up, and down
and up. There was nothing Ruby could do. She
couldn't stop Mister P pushing the buttons and
until Mister P got out, she and Leo were blocked
in. They'd be here all day if he carried on like
this.

After the third time of riding to the top floor
and back, Ruby stamped her foot.

'That's it, Mister P. ENOUGH! STOP! GET OUT!'

Mister P stuck his nose in the air and his claw hovered over 25.

'NO' said Ruby in a loud voice. 'NO, NO, NO, NO, NO!' She eyeballed the polar bear and he eyeballed her back. 'You need to start understanding a few rules if you're going to be sticking around.'

The stand-off continued for a few seconds, but eventually Mister P gave up and shuffled backwards out of the lift. Ruby stomped out of the door and down the street, Mister P stomping obediently behind. Normally Ruby would take the bus to the supermarket, but she wasn't sure if bears were allowed on buses so she decided it was better to walk. The sun blazed down and Ruby could feel the heat of the pavement through the bottom of her trainers. Poor Leo was so hot his face had turned the colour of a strawberry and Mister P's stomping got slower and slower and slower. By the time they arrived at the supermarket, all three of them were nearly cooked. But that was the least of their problems.

She stared at the sign on the door.

No dogs
except guide dogs

Mister P was already half way through the doors and there was nothing Ruby could do to stop him. She checked the sign again. It did only mention dogs. It didn't say anything about polar bears. She grabbed a trolley and followed him inside.

'OK,' she hissed. 'You push . . . and don't do anything silly.'

It started well. Bananas, potatoes, cereal, bread. Mister P wheeled the shopping trolley while Ruby checked prices and wrote down

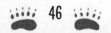

the cost next to each item to make sure she had enough to pay. Coffee, milk, apple juice, cheese, pasta, tinned tomatoes, baby food. Ruby gave a sigh of relief. Only the freezer section to go.

'Fish fingers,' she read out.

Approaching the frozen section, the air got cooler and Mister P walked with his body as close as he could to the huge freezers, trailing his nose along the edge so he could breathe in the icy atmosphere.

Ruby picked through the different brands of fish fingers, comparing prices and quantities. It took a little while because her maths wasn't brilliant. Mister P dropped his head deep into the freezer and lifted a large box of fish fingers with his teeth.

'Not that one,' said Ruby, grabbing it and putting it back.

He picked up another, then another, and then great paw-fuls at at time, chucking them into the trolley, faster and faster. Soon the trolley was piled up to overflowing and packets of frozen food started sliding onto the floor. Ruby did her best to throw stuff back into the freezer, but she couldn't keep up with Mister P's speed. Soon half the freezer was empty and he stopped.

'Have you quite finished?' she said.

Mister P kicked the trolley to one side and lifted one hairy leg over the side of the freezer. Then another.

Ruby watched in horror as

Mister P manoeuvred

his whole body

into the space where the frozen food had been.

The cold air steamed slightly as it swirled around him and he closed his eyes and sank onto his tummy with a loud 'harrumph'.

Now what? NOW WHAT?????? Leo giggled and tried to get out of his push chair to join Mister P. Ruby tried not to panic.

A small group of onlookers soon became a large crowd. The manager was called. He marched over looking very efficient, looked into the freezer, and turned a nasty shade of grey.

He tried to speak a few times but stuttered to a halt. Finally he cleared his throat and composed himself.

'Who is the owner of this polar bear?'

No one spoke. There was no way Ruby was claiming ownership of the bear. He wasn't hers. He may have gatecrashed her flat and her shopping trip, but she didn't *own* him.

'Well someone must have brought him to the supermarket. A polar bear doesn't just arrive out of nowhere,' said the manager.

'He came with me,' said Ruby quietly. 'But he's not mine.' Now all eyes were on her and Ruby *hated* being in the spotlight.

'You'll have to get him out of here.' The manager busily made some notes in a small red book. 'NO—animals—allowed—in—the— supermarket. Do you understand?' He made more notes, turning over to the next page. 'That includes polar bears . . .' he scratched his head with his pencil . . . 'I think.'

Shoppers nodded and tutted and made unhelpful comments like, 'Shouldn't be allowed.' Mister P opened one eye and closed it again, hiding his head under a large bag of frozen peas. The manager puffed out his chest.

'Now look here, *you*. Remove yourself from my freezer and leave my supermarket or I will be forced to take serious action.'

Mister P had started to snore loudly and the manager was getting angrier and angrier. Ruby knew this was serious, but she was having trouble

stopping herself from laughing.

'Poor thing,' said a voice at her shoulder. 'I suppose he must have overheated. Polar bears aren't really made for this weather.' Ruby looked at the elderly lady standing beside her. She had crinkly grey-black hair pulled back by a colourful scarf and was wearing bright orange beads.

Ruby was sure she recognized her, but there was no time to think about that now. The manager was busy counting the packets of fish fingers in Ruby's shopping trolley. 'I hope you can pay for all this food,' he said, jotting down numbers on a piece of paper. 'We can't put it back for sale now it's been handled by a bear.'

The crowd nodded their agreement.

Ruby opened her eyes wide. She didn't have anywhere near enough money to pay for it all. It'd take her weeks, months maybe, to find that sort of money. What would they do if she couldn't pay? Send her to prison? It honestly wasn't her fault that Mister P was in the freezer. It wasn't as if she'd put him there. She felt a burning sensation start in her tummy . . . the feeling she always got when things were out of control.

'Stop gawping, all of you,' she shouted, kicking a few packets of fish fingers across the floor. 'This is none of your business.

Why don't you all go and get on with your shopping and stop being so nosy?'

Everyone shuffled away, huffing and grumbling. The only person that stayed was the lady with the orange beads. 'Well said,' she whispered. 'It's so typical. All these people are quick enough to criticize, but I'd like to see

what any of them would do in your situation.'
Ruby looked at Mister P and shook her head.
What was she going to do?

'Would you like some help? It might be easier
with two of us.' The lady's brown eyes twinkled
and she gave Ruby a friendly smile.

'It's all right. I'll sort it.' Ruby picked up a
few stray boxes of fish fingers and chucked them
back into the freezer. She didn't care what that
stupid manager said.

'I've seen you at Hazeldown, haven't I?'
asked the lady. 'I think you live on the floor
above me. I'm Mrs Moresby, by the way. Nice
to meet you.'

Mrs Moresby put out her hand. Ruby wasn't
sure. She thought she'd seen Mrs Moresby
around, but she knew she shouldn't talk to
strangers and she certainly wasn't going to shake
hands.

'If I were you,' said Mrs Moresby, 'I think I'd
leave your bear . . .'

'Well, you're *not* me and this is *not* my bear!' said Ruby. Why did people think it was OK to interfere?

'All right,' Mrs Moresby continued. 'Well I just thought it might be easier if you leave the bear in the freezer for a good cool off while you go and pay and then we'll work out a way to get him home. Where does he live, by the way?'

'How would I know?' said Ruby. 'He's sleeping on our floor at the moment, but he doesn't live with us. And I can't pay, I haven't got the money.'

'Ah. Perhaps I could lend you some then?'

Ruby looked at Mrs Moresby in disbelief. 'Are you kidding me? I'm not taking your money. It's the bear's problem. It's got nothing to do with me. I'm out of here.'

Ruby sprinted out of the supermarket with Leo, leaving behind her shopping, the polar bear, and a surprised-looking Mrs Moresby.

CHAPTER 6
SECRETS AND LIES

Away from the staring faces in the supermarket, Ruby's anger melted away and she started to feel guilty. She understood Mrs Moresby was only trying to help and she shouldn't have been so rude to her. But Ruby didn't need anyone's help. People had tried to help with things before . . . like when Dad left and when Mum first got really sad. But nothing good ever seemed to come of it. As far as Ruby could see, help just made things worse.

She pushed Leo towards the bus stop. Thanks to that stupid bear, she was now in a heap of trouble and she still hadn't got any food, but at least she didn't have to walk home. Sitting on the bus, on a sunny day like today, always reminded her of Dad. In the summer holidays, while Mum was working, she and Dad used to travel all over the place for Dad to compete. On the way home, if he'd won, they'd

bubble with excitement

and she'd feel so proud to be his daughter. There wasn't much to be proud of any more. She hopped off the bus at the corner stop near Mr Jay's shop. She'd pick up the essentials, but no more. She liked Mr Jay, but his prices were a bit steep.

'I've been hoping to see you,' said Mr Jay, as he scanned Ruby's basket of items and popped them in her bag. 'I've kept a spare copy of your favourite magazine for you. It's only last month's so it's not too out of date.' He pulled a copy of **Board Talk** from under the counter and handed it to Ruby. She glanced at the skateboarder on the front cover and already her fingers itched to turn the pages. She stuffed it in the back of the pushchair.

'Thanks,' she said.

Mr Jay scanned the last item and put it into Ruby's bag. 'How's your Mum, by the way?'

'She's OK. Working. You know how it is.'

'Hmmm,' said Mr Jay. 'I haven't seen her at her workshop in ages—it looks all shut up— and I was hoping she might be able to sort out my motor. I had a bit of an argument with another car at the traffic lights earlier today. Some large animal on the road was causing all kinds of chaos and the end result is the front of my car is a mess.'

Ruby's cheeks burned. She handed over the money and waited for change. She had a nasty feeling that the animal on the road may have been a polar bear. And if Mr Jay was in need of Mum's services then it wasn't good news—or not for Mr Jay, anyway. Mum was brilliant with smashed cars. She could fix them up and have them looking good as new. She'd never been short of work, but she hadn't set foot in the workshop since Dad left . . . almost a year ago.

'I'll tell her,' said Ruby as she put the change in her pocket. 'But she's pretty busy at the moment.'

Ruby was used to lying. She had to lie to everyone—to Mr Jay, to school, to anyone she came in contact with. She couldn't tell anyone the truth about Mum's problems because Mum said that people didn't always understand and that if they thought she was too sick, they might

come and take Ruby and Leo away and split up
the whole family for ever. And Ruby was never
going to let that happen.

Ruby struggled out of the shop pushing Leo
with one hand and carrying the bag of groceries
in the other. She walked past Mr Jay's smashed-
up car. He was right, it was a mess. In one day,
that polar bear had managed to cause an awful
lot of trouble.

Ruby wondered where he was now.
Hopefully on the way back to wherever he came
from . . . or NOT . . .

As she approached her block of flats, she
noticed a large supermarket delivery truck
parked up outside. The back doors opened and
out jumped Mister P, closely followed by Mrs

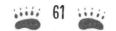

Moresby. Ruby watched in horror as the driver started unloading crate after crate of fish fingers.

She thought about trying to hide, or at least sneaking past and up to her flat. But it was too late, Mrs Moresby had spotted her.

'We made it,' said Mrs Moresby, smoothing down her dress.

'What's going on?' said Ruby.

'Well I had to get the bear out of the supermarket somehow. They said that if I paid for the fish fingers, they'd deliver them and the bear for free. Mister P seemed very nervous about getting into the van so I decided I'd better travel with him. It was quite a journey.'

'You paid for all the shopping?' Ruby knew she needed to act fast and get it all taken away. She hated to think what it had cost. She marched up to the driver. 'We don't need this delivery, thank you. You can take it all back. The bear too, if you like.'

'I'm not putting that bear back in my van,' said the driver, 'I've never been so terrified in all my life. And the rest is signed and paid for.' He slammed the back door with a loud bang, got into the driver's seat, and skidded off at high speed.

Ruby stared at the pile of frozen food on the pavement and at the truck disappearing into the distance.

'What are we going to do with it all,' she said, looking first at Mister P and then at Mrs Moresby. 'Our freezer isn't even working.'

'I can hold on to it for you,' said Mrs Moresby. 'I have a large freezer in my flat which never gets used. I've been meaning to get rid of it.'

'But who is going to eat it? You don't really think Mister P is going to stay, do you?'

'I rather think he might,' said Mrs Moresby.

Ruby tried to think straight. It was true that there was no point in wasting all this food, but she couldn't imagine where she was ever going to find the money to pay back Mrs Moresby. She had no idea how long the bear was planning to stay . . . or even if he had a plan at all. If she started feeding him, maybe it would just encourage him to stick around and she certainly didn't want that. Then again, she could hardly let him starve. She hid her face in her hands. She didn't know where to turn.

'Don't worry too much,' said Mrs Moresby.

'I'm happy to help.'

'I don't need your charity, if that's what you're thinking,' said Ruby.

Mrs Moresby sighed. 'I'm just offering. I didn't mean to cause offence.'

Ruby knew she should be grateful to Mrs Moresby, but what if she could never repay her? Ruby didn't need that kind of worry at the moment. **She didn't need a polar bear either,** come to that.

'I suppose you'd like help getting all this to your flat?' said Ruby, sighing. Leo was beginning to grizzle.

Mrs Moresby shook her head. 'I think you should get your baby brother and Mister P out of the sun. I've called my grandson and he is on his way over to give me a hand. We'll be fine.' Mrs Moresby waved them away. 'And Ruby,' she said calling after them, 'You can send your bear down any time he needs a snack.'

'He's not my bear,' said Ruby. 'He really

isn't. But thanks.' Ruby tried to smile, but she doubted it looked very convincing.

'You seem to have made a friend,' she said to Mister P as they travelled up in the lift. Her shoulders drooped and she gave a sad laugh. 'Everyone finds it easy to make friends except me.'

CHAPTER 7
FRIENDS AND ENEMIES

'Ruby Holton, you know you're not allowed to use your mobile phone in class. This isn't the first time I've had to remind you.'

Ruby didn't have time to read the text from Mum before Miss Dennis, her teacher, swept past her desk and scooped up her mobile phone. 'No mobile phones without permission. You know the rules.'

'But I DO have permission. I've told you before. You checked, remember?'

'You do not have permission to use your phone in my lesson.'

'But it might be an important message from Mum.'

'The only important message from your mum should be to concentrate on your work like everybody else.'

Ruby was too tired to concentrate on anything. She'd been awake half the night worrying about Mum and Mister P and how she was going to get the money to pay back Mrs Moresby. Mum, at least, was beginning to get used to Mister P and she'd waved Ruby off to school this morning telling her she'd be fine. But Mum's version of fine and Ruby's version of fine were two different things, and she'd made Mum promise to text her if there was a problem.

Ruby thumped her book on the table.

'No need for that,' said Miss Dennis. 'I'm sure your mum can wait until you get home to talk to you.'

Miss Dennis had no idea. She didn't know anything. Ruby tried to focus on the page of science in front of her but everything seemed blurry and confused. She rubbed her eyes.

'Cry baby,' hissed Kelly.

'I am NOT crying,' said Ruby.

'You so are,' said Kelly.

That was it! The worry inside Ruby boiled over as red-hot anger and she picked up her science book and threw it at Kelly.

Kelly screamed and a buzz of gasps and laughter went round the class.

Miss Dennis looked at Ruby for a long time and then pointed at the door. 'Outside, Ruby. Take your work.'

Ruby opened the door of the classroom and made her way to her usual desk in the corridor. Ruby was always being sent out of class. Sometimes, Ruby thought, it was better out here away from everyone else.

Of course, at break time she had to see Miss Dennis and apologize to Kelly. She hated Kelly, but she knew she shouldn't have thrown a book at her. The rest of the day no one wanted to sit near her. She'd like to have apologized to Zena too—but even she was avoiding Ruby and whispering with the others.

At home time, she picked up her phone from the office, only to find it was out of battery so she couldn't even check her messages. She walked home as fast as she could, took the lift to the 22nd floor, and opened the door.

Straight away, she knew things were bad.

***

The flat was hot and airless. Leo was standing at the bars of his playpen, tears streaming down

his snotty face, his nappy so soggy that it was hanging half way down his little legs. Mister P was pacing around the flat looking flustered and there was no sign of Mum.

Ruby pushed Mum's bedroom door open. The room was in darkness. It was scary when Mum was like this. It was the worst.

'Mum?'

No answer.

'Mum? MUM!'

Mister P came and stood beside her and put his paw on her shoulder. It was a large paw, but it felt comfortable.

'Wake up, Mum,' said Ruby more gently.

'Where have you been?' Mum's voice was just a whisper, 'I tried to call you.'

Ruby closed her eyes as relief washed over her. She always panicked when she couldn't wake Mum up.

'Miss Dennis confiscated my phone, but I'm here now. Don't worry.'

Leo's angry cries were getting louder and Mum put her hands over her ears.

'I'll get Leo sorted,' said Ruby. 'I expect he needs feeding.'

Ruby had learnt that she couldn't do much to help when Mum was like this. The best thing was to look after everything else and let Mum rest as much as possible.

Ruby flung open the door to the balcony and picked up Leo.

'Yuck,' she said and tickled his tummy.

Mister P put both paws over his nose and turned his head away while Ruby sorted Leo's nappy. Then she settled her little brother in his chair with his beaker and some food.

Mister P's tummy rumbled loudly. 'I suppose you're hungry too,' said Ruby, sighing. She knew she'd have no choice but to pay a visit to Mrs Moresby to let Mister P raid her freezer.

Ruby finished feeding Leo then counted out the change left over in Mum's purse. Then the three of them made their way down to the 21st floor. Ruby wasn't sure which flat was Mrs Moresby's, but Mister P had his nose down on the floor and sniffed his way confidently towards 21c.

'You'd better be right,' Ruby said as she pressed the buzzer. 'Otherwise we're in

BIG trouble.'

The door opened and, much to Ruby's relief, there was Mrs Moresby, a huge smile spread across her face. 'You found me!' she said.

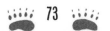

'Mister P found you,' said Ruby.

'Well, I suppose if you're used to hunting your prey in the ocean, it's not going to be that hard to find your fish fingers in a block of flats.' She laughed a big, bright laugh. 'Would you like to come in?'

Ruby hesitated. She hardly knew Mrs Moresby. Mister P gave her a hard shove with his nose and the next thing she knew she was in the middle of Mrs Moresby's living room. Ruby

glowered at the bear. She'd be having words with him later.

Everything in Mrs Moresby's flat was bright and tidy, just like Mrs Moresby herself. The flat had a friendly feel with lots of photographs on all the surfaces. Ruby couldn't help noticing a picture of a boy doing a trick, maybe a kickflip, on his skateboard.

Mrs Moresby followed her gaze. 'That's my grandson,' she said. 'He loves his skateboarding.'

Ruby felt a lump of jealousy in her throat.

'I haven't really got much time,' said Ruby. 'I need some food for Mister P.'

Mister P had positioned himself close to the kitchen door, right by her freezer, and was staring at Mrs Moresby in a hopeful way.

'How many packets would he like, do you think?' asked Mrs Moresby. Mister P's eyes danced over the piles of fish fingers.

'I've only got money for eight,' said Ruby, 'Do you think that will be enough?'

'Enough for today, perhaps,' said Mrs Moresby laughing again. 'Unfortunately, I think you might find that polar bears have quite an appetite.' She counted out eight packets and emptied them into a large plastic tub.

'Don't we need to cook them?' Ruby asked.

'I wouldn't have thought so,' said Mrs Moresby. 'Polar bears are used to cold and ice. It doesn't look as though he's fussy.'

Mister P already had his nose in the tub and they watched in fascination as Mister P tossed a fish finger in the air and caught it in his mouth.

Leo clapped his hands and Mister P did it again and again.

'He's a bit of a juggler, your bear,' said Mrs Moresby.

Ruby folded her arms.

'Sorry,' said Mrs Moresby. 'I know, he is

NOT
your
bear.'

It had been a long day but, in spite of everything, Ruby found she had quite enjoyed her visit to Mrs Moresby and part of her didn't want to go back home. Still, she shouldn't leave Mum for too long and she needed to eat too— and tidy up—and get Leo ready for bed—and do her homework. The list of things to do was always so long. She said goodbye to Mrs Moresby and climbed the stairs back home.

Ruby took Mum a sandwich and a cup of tea and she and Leo sat with her for a while. Mum sipped at her tea, but ignored the sandwich

so Ruby ended up eating it herself. Then she dragged Leo's cot into her own bedroom so he wouldn't disturb Mum in the night. It was quite late by the time she pulled on the old T-shirt she slept in and folded her uniform ready for the morning. Now there was only her reading homework left to do.

She picked up her book. 'The Secret Life of Polar Bears' it said on the front. She'd chosen it during library time today because she thought it might be useful. She went to the index to see if there was anything about polar bears and hot-air balloons, but nothing was mentioned so she turned to the first page and started reading. *'Polar bears live in the Arctic Circle,'* she read aloud, quietly. She raised her eyebrows. *Not this one,* she thought as a long furry nose poked round her bedroom door. *'They are solitary creatures,'* she read as Mister P pushed his way into her room and squeezed into the gap between her bed and the wall on the opposite side to Leo's cot. 'Solitary,' she repeated and looked at Mister P.

Mister P blinked and settled himself with his head on the bed beside her. Ruby rolled her eyes. 'Well this is going to be a cosy night,' she said. 'Do we not think it might be a bit crowded for a *solitary* creature with THREE in this bedroom?'

Mister P shifted himself from side to side until he was nice and comfortable.

'Hmm,' said Ruby. *'They are well adapted to a life in the snow and ice.'*

Ruby put down the book and looked at Mister P. 'You're a long way from home, Mister P. Are you in trouble or something? Otherwise, what are you doing here?'

Mister P stared out of the window. Little pin-pricks of light twinkled in his deep black eyes. Ruby smiled. 'Did you know you've got the night sky in your eyes?'

Mister P closed his eyes slowly and started to snore. Ruby lifted his head gently off the bed and placed it on the floor. She'd had enough of her book. She didn't think there was anything very secret about what it told her. She could write a far better version.

She turned off her light and lay in the darkness, but her mind was too busy with worries. Sometimes it was hard to know what to do with all this worry. At home she was careful to keep it all inside, but at school sometimes, like today, it all overflowed like a big angry roar and there was nothing she could do to control it.

'I'm not really a nasty person, Mister P. Everyone says I am . . . but I'm not, you know.'

Mister P snored loudly. It was easy to talk to a sleeping polar bear, thought Ruby, though he wasn't much good at giving answers. She gave up trying to sleep, switched on the light again and picked up her copy of BOard Talk magazine. She flicked through the pages to distract herself with all the wonderful pictures and stories. She wished Dad was still here, she wished she could be a champion skater, she wished Mum would be better in the morning and that all her worries, including a large snoring polar bear, could go away.

CHAPTER 8

PROBLEMS AND SOLUTIONS

B-B-Bip. B-B-Bip. B-B-BIP.

The sound of her alarm dragged Ruby from a deep sleep and she wondered if the city was in the grip of an earthquake. Her room was shaking and there was a loud thunk, thunk, thunk close to her ear. She stuck out her hand towards the clock. Why did it feel furry? And why was Leo laughing?

She slowly opened her eyes and the day

crashed in on her. Oh great! So the polar bear was definitely still here. In fact, he was perched on the edge of her bed smacking the alarm clock as hard as he could with his front paw. Leo was bouncing up and down in his cot, giggling for all he was worth.

Ruby tried to grab the alarm clock. 'It's 6.30 in the morning! Give me a break.'

Mister P dropped the shattered alarm clock onto the floor and Ruby covered her head with her duvet and took a few deep breaths before clambering off the end of her bed. She left the chaos of her bedroom and went through to Mum.

'Morning,' said Ruby, trying to sound chirpy as she opened Mum's curtains. 'It's a lovely sunny day.'

Mum barely moved. Ruby could see she was awake, but she was staring at the wall almost as if she couldn't see Ruby at all. Ruby sometimes wished she could see what was going on in

Mum's head. If only Mum would talk to her, she might be able to help. A wave of hopelessness nearly drowned Ruby as she tried to work out what she should do for the best.

'Do you think we should get the doctor?' she asked.

Mum shook her head and felt for Ruby's hand. Silent tears ran down her face. 'I don't need the doctor. I'll be OK soon. Don't you worry.'

Don't worry? DON'T WORRY?! Ruby bottled up her shout inside her. How was she supposed not to worry?

'I'll stay home today, shall I?' said Ruby. 'I'll send a note to school off your computer? I'll say I'm sick again, shall I?'

Mum nodded. Ruby closed the door to Mum's room and it felt like shutting her troubles away. Leo was crying gently and Ruby lifted him out of his cot held him close.

'Don't cry,' she whispered. 'I'll look after

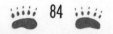

you and I promise, *promise*, that no one will
ever take us away from Mum. Not ever. We'll be
OK, you'll see.'

At that moment, Ruby felt a huge pair of hairy
arms wrap all the way around her and Leo,
embracing them in a massive hug.

It caught her off guard and for a second
she thought she might cry too.

But there was no time for feeling sorry for herself and she pushed Mister P away.

'It's too hot for that,' she said clearing her throat. 'And we need to get on with the day. Here, you can make yourself useful.'

Ruby sat Leo in between Mister P's two front paws and watched as Leo tried to grab the end of Mister P's nose. Mister P soon got the hang of the game and played along. Ruby smiled as she watched them and wondered what excuse to use in her absence note today. She'd already used doctors' appointments, dentists' appointments, Grandmother's illness, and chicken pox. She'd once tried asthma but then her teachers started asking her about inhalers. She sat at Mum's laptop.

To: absences@St.Thomasschool.edu.org

Subject: Ruby Holton: ABSENCE

I regret that Ruby will be absent from school today. She has a high fever and is on medications. She may be away for a few days until she is fully recovered as we don't want to pass on anything nasty.

Lisa Holton

Ruby read and re-read the email and pressed SEND. She thought it sounded pretty good. School probably wouldn't believe a word of it, but there wasn't much they could do. Fever was the best excuse and it gave her a reason to be off for a few days. She'd be missing the trip to the museum, but that was too bad.

She boiled the kettle and started to make breakfast. On the telly, a teenage boy was being interviewed. He was only 14 but, apparently, he'd caused a big sensation busking on the streets, playing his saxophone. Now he was off to a special music school. The interview switched to a clip of him playing and people putting money into a basket at his feet. Ruby turned up the volume.

Mister P pressed his ear to the TV and started to swing his backside left and right in time with the music.

'Move yourself, Mister P,' said Ruby. 'I want to watch.'

Mister P **bounced** from paw to paw then finally stood up on one leg and **spun around,** hitting his head on the light bulb and losing his balance.

Ruby leapt across the room, caught a mug as it fell off the table, and steadied the TV as it wobbled on its stand. 'For goodness' sake,' she said. 'Take it easy. And where on earth did you learn to dance like that?'

The music came to an end and the camera panned in on the basket of notes and coins. He must be nearly a millionaire and it all looked so simple: Stand on the street, play a tune, and earn lots of money. Problem solved! She could do that! The only issue, as Ruby saw it, was that she didn't play the saxophone—or any other instrument. She wondered if she still had Gramps's mouth organ somewhere. She rummaged around in her bottom drawer until she discovered it, wrapped in yellow tissue paper.

She tried a few notes, blowing gently into the old instrument and sliding it backwards and forwards across her lips. She blew a little harder. Leo put his hands over his ears and screwed his eyes tight shut. Mister P hid his head under a cushion.

It wasn't going well. Ruby threw the mouth

organ onto the chair.

Knock, knock, knock.

Ruby stood rooted to the spot. Mum had told her NEVER to let anyone in because you never knew who it might be.

Knock, knock, knock. Louder this time.

Ruby went to the door. 'Who is it?' she shouted.

'It's Mrs Moresby. What on earth are you doing in there?'

Ruby breathed a sigh of relief and opened the door a crack, without taking it off its chain.

'It sounded as though you were about to come through the ceiling,' whispered Mrs Moresby. 'You'll be getting complaints from the neighbours.'

'It was only Mister P dancing. There's no law against that, is there?'

Mrs Moresby raised her eyebrows. 'There are no laws against dancing, but there are laws against having animals in the building and making too much noise. I suggest Mister P tries to be a little lighter on his feet.' Mrs Moresby looked around her, checking left and right.

'You won't tell anyone,' said Ruby, 'About Mister P, I mean.'

'Of course I won't. Your secret it safe with me and, to prove it, I've brought him some breakfast. I thought it might help quieten things down.' She tried to push a couple of packets of fish fingers through the gap, but Ruby stopped her.

'I can't take them,' said Ruby. 'Not until I can pay you.'

'These are a gift from me to Mister P. We'll sort out the rest later. But you could let me in. That might make things easier.'

Ruby shook her head. Letting Mrs Moresby in would not make things easier. 'Mum doesn't like strangers in the house,' she said, her eyes flicking in the direction of Mum's room.

Mrs Moresby fiddled with her orange beads. 'Perhaps you could introduce me to your mum, if she's here, and then I wouldn't be a stranger any more.'

'I can't,' said Ruby, 'She's got the flu.' This was getting complicated. It was time for Mrs Moresby to go back downstairs.

'Ruby, I hope you don't mind me asking, but shouldn't you be at school?'

Ruby did mind her asking. Mrs Moresby was beginning to make her feel uncomfortable.

'I'm getting the flu too. And so is Mister P. It's a very nasty one, so I wouldn't come too close.' At the sound of his name, Mister P skidded to the door and Ruby managed to

slam

it closed just in time. She didn't need Mister P getting involved in this conversation.

'Now look at what you've gone and done,' she said, turning to Mister P. 'We don't need people poking around up here and sticking their noses into our business. We DON'T need to draw attention to ourselves.'

Ruby slid down the door and sat on the floor. She tucked the boxes of fish fingers behind her back and looked up at the polar bear towering above her. It was pretty hard not to draw attention to yourself—the wrong sort of attention—if you had a polar bear in your home. She blew a few more notes on the mouth organ.

'I hope you don't mind me asking,' she said, 'but how long are you planning to stay—exactly?'

Mister P started to tap his paw to the sound of the mouth organ. Leo squawked from his playpen.

'**Shhhh,**' said Ruby, 'both of you, or we'll have Mrs Moresby back on the doorstep.'

Ruby continued to play a tuneless rise and fall of notes, as thoughts went round and round. She knew Mrs Moresby was right. She should be at school. And she wished she hadn't been so rude because Mrs Moresby had been kind to her and was only trying to help. It was just easier to keep people away—especially when they started asking questions.

But an idea was beginning to form in her head. If she could pay back Mrs Moresby then that would solve one problem. Then it was just a matter of getting Mum back on her feet . . . and going back to a school where she had no friends . . . and getting a noisy polar bear out of her flat . . .

She stopped playing, but Mister P wouldn't stop dancing. Ruby kicked out at his paw and he jumped away and continued to jig.

'Stop it! Please! You're going to get us thrown out.'

Bang, bang, bang went Mister P's paws on the hard floor.

'SHUT UP!' shouted Ruby and flung the mouth organ at Mister P in frustration.

It hit him on the nose and he whimpered and lay down quietly, cradling his nose in his paws.

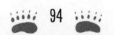 94

Ruby hung her head. 'I'm sorry,' she mumbled, 'But sometimes you are such a pain.'

Mister P got to his feet, retrieved the fish fingers from by the door, turned his back and walked out onto the balcony.

Ruby waited a few minutes, waiting for her anger to simmer down, then followed him out.

'This is what happens,' she said. 'I always end up throwing something at somebody. I don't seem to be able to help it.'

Mister P looked at her wisely then, with
a deep sigh, lay down. Ruby sat down next
to the bear and he let her rest her head
against his side. She ran her hand gently
down his fur, over and over until slowly
they both started to relax and close their
eyes. Ruby wished they could stay here
all day, just her and Mister P chilling out
together on the balcony. But there was too
much to do and Leo had started to squawk
in his playpen, demanding her attention.

Dear Dad

Leo and me have got a friend staying. He's a polar bear. I'm not lying. His name is Mister P and he's all right most of the time, though he is rather large and noisy and annoying. The biggest problem is that he eats a lot and that gets expensive. I don't want to bother Mum for the money so I'm thinking of busking. What do you reckon? Top tips for playing the mouth organ would be appreciated.

Anyway, it's my birthday in two days' time. I haven't got anything planned yet, but if you wanted to come round and meet Mister P then we could have a party. I think Mum and Leo would like to see you.

Love Ruby

Ruby held her letter up to the sky. She'd spent the afternoon trying to improve her musical skills while Mister P had entertained Leo. Or maybe Leo had entertained Mister P, She wasn't quite sure. Anyway, Ruby reckoned her mouth organ playing was much improved and soon she'd be ready to perform in public. She just needed to find the time and place to do it. Maybe tomorrow would be the day?

CHAPTER 9
MOVING
AND GROOVING

Ruby never had any idea, from one day to the
next, how Mum was going to be. This morning
Ruby awoke to the sound of the radio on full-
volume and Mum vacuuming the flat to within
an inch of its life. The combination of the heat
and all this activity had turned the flat into an
oven. Ruby opened every window as wide as
she could. She sometimes wondered if Mum's
VERY BUSY days were almost worse than the
days when Mum didn't want to get out of bed.

'You need to get this bear out of my house,' Mum shouted over the noise. 'I've never seen so much white hair. It's like living in a zoo.' Mum pointed the nozzle at Mister P and his fur flowed in long white waves towards the suction hose. Mister P backed off, showing his teeth and growling.

'He needs space,' yelled Mum, 'And so do I.'

Ruby hit the switch on the vacuum. It was doing her head in and she didn't want Mrs Moresby back on her doorstep complaining about the noise and asking more tricky questions.

'Perhaps we could all go out,' suggested Ruby. Getting Mum out of the flat often seemed to help Mum's mood and today seemed like the perfect opportunity. They could all go to the park. She wanted to see if Mister P's hot-air balloon was still there. She hoped it was, then she could prove to Mum that she hadn't been making it up.

'I can't possibly go out,' said Mum. 'I've got far too much to do.' She pressed the "on" button of the vacuum again. 'And Leo seems a bit off colour. I don't think he should go anywhere so I'll keep him here with me.'

Mum was right about Leo. He'd woken up with a snotty nose and hadn't been interested in his breakfast. Now he was sleeping, in spite of all the noise.

Ruby dressed as quickly as she could. If Mum wasn't going to venture out, then this could be her chance to give busking a go. But she'd need to be careful. She didn't want Mum to get suspicious and she couldn't risk being seen or someone might tell school.

Ruby had already been thinking about the best place to go and she'd settled on the Highcross Shopping Centre. It was a place she used to go with Dad—mainly because it had a big skateboarding shop—and she reckoned it was far enough away from home to be safe.

There were always loads of people around and she thought she remembered seeing buskers there before.

She slipped on her dark glasses and pulled the rim of her cap down over her face. That way, even if she bumped into someone she knew, they shouldn't recognize her. Mister P inspected her closely and walked to the table where Mum had thrown her own dark glasses. He picked them up delicately in his teeth.

'Hey, you can't take those,' shouted Mum, switching off the vacuum. 'Come back!' But Mister P let himself out the door and started running down the stairs. Ruby followed him, laughing. When they arrived at the bottom, out of breath, Ruby took the glasses from Mister P's teeth and balanced them carefully on his nose. 'Very cool,' she said.

It was too far to walk to Highcross so Ruby had to hope that Mister P would be OK on the bus. She needn't have worried. He smiled at the driver, and took care not to bump into the other passengers, before settling down in the aisle. He sat quietly staring out the window and watching the city race by. Ruby was interested . . . it was almost as though he always travelled by bus!

'Done this before, have you?' asked Ruby as they reached their stop and climbed off.

Mister P raised his paw as if to say goodbye to the other passengers. A couple of them waved back and Ruby puffed out her cheeks. 'You're full of surprises,' she said.

As they made their way towards the shopping centre, Ruby nervously fingered the mouth organ in her pocket. She tried to imagine herself busking and it made her tummy feel funny—sort of sick and jumpy all at the same time. She wondered if busking was such a good idea after all. She slowed her steps and came to a stop in front of the skateboard shop.

The window was full of shiny new skateboards and a TV was playing clips of boarders doing insane tricks. She'd like to have gone in, like she used to with Dad, but it made her feel kind of sad being back here.

'Dad said he'd give me one of these for my birthday, one day,' she said. 'If I could choose, I think that's the one I'd like.' She pointed to a slick-looking board painted bright blue. 'What do you think?'

Mister P was busy watching the TV screen. Ruby could see the colours reflected in his shiny eyes. A girl walked out with a huge package under her arm and Ruby tried to imagine what that would feel like—walking out with a brand new skateboard of your very own. Like that would ever happen. She'd have to busk for about a hundred years before she had enough money for a skateboard.

Ruby needed to stop dreaming and remember what she'd come here for. She needed money to pay Mrs Moresby before she could even think about saving for anything else.

'Come on,' she said to Mister P. 'Let's get this over and done with.'

She found what she thought was good spot, pulled the mouth organ out of her pocket, and took a deep breath. Her mouth felt dry and sticky as she tried the first few notes. This was harder than she thought. Somehow, out here in the shopping centre, the mouth organ sounded like a car crash. People walked past her, but no one took any notice. How dare they ignore her! Ruby could feel herself getting more and more wound up. And the more angry Ruby got, the worse her playing sounded. People were actually going out of their way to avoid her.

'Don't just stand there, Mister P,

DO SOMETHING,'

she hissed.

Mister P looked left and looked right. He quietly removed the cap from Ruby's head and put it on the ground. Ruby panicked. Now

everybody could see her face! Then Mister P grabbed the mouth organ, stuck it between his teeth, and blew. His playing, if you could call it that, was even worse than Ruby's. But then he started to hop from

foot to foot, wiggling his bum and turning circles. Ruby took a few steps back and it wasn't long before the first coin dropped into the cap, closely followed by another. Soon coins were flying through the air, clinking and clattering as the pile increased. Ruby wasn't surprised; it was the funniest thing she'd ever seen and Mister P seemed to be enjoying every minute.

Soon a small crowd had gathered in a circle around him and they'd started to dance along with him. Ruby danced too.

Everytime Mister P stopped, they clapped and shouted,

MORE!

MORE!

ENCORE!

ENCORE!

Ruby looked at the money in the hat. If Mister P carried on like this, they'd pay Mrs Moresby back in no time at all. But now the crowd was getting larger and Ruby worried that things might be getting a bit out of hand. She didn't want any trouble and she knew what happened when Mister P got overheated.

'That's enough for today, Mister P,' she said firmly, 'We need to leave.'

'We want more, we want more!'

chanted the crowd.

'Come on,' said Ruby, trying to drag Mister P away. 'Let's quit while the going's good.'

Out of the corner of her eye she thought she saw a policeman coming round the corner and she had a feeling a policeman might not be so impressed with a busking polar bear. She grabbed the mouth organ from Mister P, picked up her cap, and ran through the crowd. Mister P galloped along behind her and in no time at all they were racing out of Highcross towards the bus stop. A bus was just pulling in. 'Quick!' shouted Ruby, leaping on and holding the door. Mister P squeezed on behind her, the doors hissed closed, and they collapsed into a seat, gasping for breath.

'We did it, Mister P,' she said as they peeped into the hat. Most of the money was small change, but there must be almost enough to pay back Mrs Moresby. Ruby laughed. It all felt like a bit of an adventure and it had been fun going out and doing something different. It was good to have a break every now and again. But now she was ready to get home. She didn't like to leave Mum for too long.

She let the coins run through her hands.

'Good job, Mister P. Fish fingers for tea!'

CHAPTER 10
DUCKING AND DIVING

Ruby arrived back to the cleanest, tidiest flat she'd ever seen, but there was no sign of Mum or Leo. She knew there was no real reason to worry, but a sense of unease nibbled away at her.

Leo's pushchair wasn't there so that meant they must have gone out.

The excitement of the shopping centre suddenly seemed very distant. They took off their dark glasses, tipped the money into a plastic bag, and hid it under the bed. Then they headed for the park.

Mister P sniffed the ground as they walked down the street. He kept going through the park, slowing a little as he passed the place where his balloon had landed. There was no sign of it now and he continued until the edge of the pond came into view.

'There they are,' said Ruby, pointing towards Mum and Leo. 'You're good with that nose of yours.'

She stood and watched them from a distance. Mum was crouched down next to Leo's pushchair. It was such a happy sight to see them out together. It looked so normal.

Mum stood up when she saw them coming.

'I thought you said you weren't going out,' said Ruby.

'I changed my mind. Leo's been a right little toad all day.'

Ruby bent down over the push chair. 'Aw . . . look at your nose,' she said. 'It's horrible.'

'He's been snivelling like that since you left.

He must be teething, poor mite,' said Mum.

Ruby stroked Leo's cheek. It was hot and pink. Mister P stared into the pond.

'You should go in for a swim, Mister P,' said Mum. 'It might help get rid of some of that excess hair of yours.'

'What, and then take him back to our sparkling clean flat,' said Ruby. 'I don't think so. Look at the colour of the pond!'

'But he's built to swim,' said Mum. *'Ursus Maritimus.'* She pronounced the words like a magic spell.

'Ursus WHAT?'

'Latin for sea bear,' Mum said. 'That's what it says in your book. I was reading it to Leo this morning.'

Mister P dipped one paw into the water, sending ripples skidding across the surface. He was concentrating hard. Suddenly he launched himself into the water with an enormous

splash

and reappeared with a large fish flip-flopping in his mouth.

Ruby gasped. 'NO, Mister P! You can't eat the fish from the pond. Put it back. Drop it. Drop it now.'

Mister P did drop it . . . straight down into his tummy.

'Mum! That's horrible. Do something!'

'I suppose it's only natural,' said Mum. '

'Not here in the park it's not. What if someone sees?' Ruby looked around, but there was no one about. She watched as Mister P turned onto his stomach and swam smoothly away. He rolled and splashed and played in the water and finally waded out onto the grass. Long strands of slimy pond weed hung across his nose, making him look more green bear than polar bear, and muddy-grey water streamed off his fur into a puddle on the ground beneath him.

Mister P hunched his shoulders.

'We need to move,' said Ruby, suddenly

clocking what was about to happen. But she was too late. Mister P shook and shook until the three of them were splattered with murky pond water.

'My clean clothes,' said Mum, wiping her hands down her T-shirt. Leo rubbed water out of his eyes with his little fists and Ruby pulled off her cap and did her best to shoo Mister P away.

'Did anyone ever tell you you're a pain in the neck?' Ruby asked angrily. 'We're doing our best to look after you and then you go and do THIS!' She pointed to herself and Mister P sat down, tipped his head to one side and pointed to himself with a large paw.

'Yes, YOU,' said Ruby. 'You with the big, wet, smelly-pond-water body. *Ursus-pain-in-the-neckus.* That's what you should be called.' Ruby thumped her cap back on her head. 'Right, come on. We'll have to go to the playground while we all dry off. We can't take Mister P back to the flat like this, he'll wreck the place.'

Mum hung back. 'I'm not sure I'm up to visiting the playground yet. There are always so many people there.'

Ruby often thought that the real reason Mum didn't like going to the playground was because it was next to the skatepark and the skatepark reminded her of Dad. But Mum couldn't avoid these things forever.

'It'll be OK. Most people will be picking up their kids from school now. We don't need to be long—just time to dry off.'

Ruby coaxed Mum towards the swings. The playground was more or less deserted, which was good, but the skatepark was chock full of older kids. Ruby felt that familiar twinge of jealousy as she breathed in the excitement and adrenaline. Wheels on concrete—the sound she dreamed of.

She helped Mum get Leo into the swing then waved Mister P over to the roundabout. It was the perfect spin dryer for a wet polar bear.

Mister P eyed it suspiciously.

'Don't worry, it's fun. Climb on!'

Mister P clambered on carefully, wrapping his claws around the metal handles. Ruby started scooting it round. It took a while to get going; it was heavy with a polar bear on top, but soon Mister P got the idea and scooted with her.

Faster and faster they went until they were spinning at dizzying speed and Mister P was grinning for all he was worth. He clung on until the roundabout slowed to a stop, then slid off into a heap on the ground. He tried to get up, but his legs were all over the place. When he regained his balance enough to stand, he staggered in the direction of the skatepark and collapsed with his front paws draped over the wall.

Ruby clambered up Mister P's back so she could get a bird's eye view of the skaters.

'It looks cool, doesn't it?' she said, whispering down his ear. Mister P was hypnotized. His nose went up and down and side to side as he followed the boards backwards and forwards.

In her mind, Ruby could see herself riding the skaters she was watching. axle stalls and drop-ins, just like the skaters she was watching.

'I'm going to be there one day,' she said, scratching Mister P's head between his ears. 'You wait and see.'

She slid back down Mister P's back.

She'd do it, she knew she would.

It was in her blood.

CHAPTER 11

HAPPY AND SAD

Happy birthday to me,
happy birthday to me . . .

Ruby's voice trailed off. The tune sounded so
sad that she had to stop. How did most eleven-
year-olds spend their birthdays? Not like
this. No, most people had cards and cakes and
presents. She stared around the flat. No sign of
any birthday surprises at all.

She sighed, took the last biscuit from the
packet of custard creams, and plonked herself
on the floor next to Mister P. 'I wonder when

your birthday is?' she said to him. 'You could share mine if you like—not that there's much to share.' She passed half the biscuit to Mister P and he nibbled at it in a very un-polar-bearish way.

She was glad Mister P was here. Yesterday had been such a good day and she'd thought Mum had turned the corner. But today Mum was too tired to get out of bed and she hadn't even mentioned the word birthday.

Worse still, Leo had kept Ruby up half the night snuffling and coughing and fussing with his sore teeth. And now, just when she needed to give him his breakfast, he refused to wake up.

She edged closer to Mister P, feeling the softness of his fur and the reassurance of his steady breathing. On days like this, Ruby's world seemed to shrink very small and she felt trapped in the flat with all her problems. She'd like to escape and clamber into the basket of Mister P's hot-air balloon and float high above the rooftops without a care in the world. But that's not how life worked.

Ruby jumped up as she heard a terrible sound from Leo's cot. It was somewhere between a cough and a bark. Ruby rushed to her room and put her hand against Leo's forehead and felt the burning heat. She knew, immediately, that this was much more than a problem with his teeth. Leo was sick.

Mister P put his head round the door, took one look at Leo, and skidded through to Mum's room. The next thing Ruby knew, he'd got the bottom of Mum's T-shirt between his teeth and

was dragging her towards Leo's cot.

Mum lifted Leo into her arms. She felt his head, his legs, his tummy. 'Oh no, oh no!' she moaned, over and over. She started rushing around opening and closing cupboards and drawers. 'I'm sure I've got medicine somewhere, I bought some . . . oh, I don't know . . . some time!' Poor Leo started crying and coughing uncontrollably and Mum didn't seem to know what direction to go in next.

Leo's eyes looked all wrong and he was getting more and more distressed. Suddenly Mum handed Leo to Ruby and ran for the bathroom. Ruby could hear the unmistakable sounds of Mum throwing up. Ruby was desperate. She needed help and she needed help fast. Mister P was turning circles and scratching at the front door and suddenly Ruby understood.

She opened the door and, quick as a flash, Mister P was off down the stairs.

Ruby heard banging and then the sound of Mrs Moresby's voice.

'All right Mister P. I'm coming, I'm coming. Keep your hair on.'

Mrs Moresby arrived in the flat at high speed, helped along by a good shove from Mister P. She looked around and took in the situation.

'It's all right, Ruby,' she said, 'don't you worry.' She took Leo out of Ruby's arms and smiled at him. 'You're a little bit warm, aren't you young man.' She started to remove his clothes until he was wearing only his nappy and she put two fingers against his chest and looked at her watch.

'Ruby, could you go and find me a sponge and a bowl of cool water. There's a good girl. Mister P, it might be best if you stayed out of the way.'

Ruby came back with the bowl and sponge

and Mrs Moresby started to dab Leo's body with cool water.

'Is your mum here?' she asked.

Ruby nodded towards the bathroom door.

'Here,' said Mrs Moresby handing Ruby the sponge. 'You keep Leo cool, I'll go and check on her. Would that be OK?

Ruby nodded.

'What's her name?'

'Lisa,' said Ruby. 'But most people call her Liss.'

Ruby held the cool sponge against Leo's forehead. Mrs Moresby knocked on the bathroom door then let herself in. Ruby listened as Mrs Moresby spoke quietly to Mum.

'Hello Lisa. I'm Josephine Moresby and I'm a neighbour from one floor down. Are you feeling all right?'

Ruby heard Mum mumble something and sob.

'I know,' said Mrs Moresby. 'It is such a

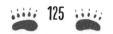

worry when little ones are sick. But I'm a retired nurse so I've seen plenty of it in my time and Leo is going to be fine. There's a nasty bug doing the rounds, but he looks like a tough little man so I'm sure he'll be over it soon. Why don't you take a few moments to sort yourself out and I'll go and put the kettle on for a nice cup of tea.'

Ruby closed her eyes. She liked the sound of Mrs Moresby's voice and she was glad Mrs Moresby was here to help. It made things so much easier when there was someone who knew what to do, someone to share the worry with. She looked at Mister P sitting in the corner. If it hadn't been for him, she never would have met Mrs Moresby. Perhaps having a polar bear to stay wasn't so bad after all.

'Do you know if your mum takes any medication,' asked Mrs Moresby coming out of the bathroom.

Ruby nodded and went to fetch the bottle of pills. She handed it to Mrs Moresby. 'I don't know if she's taken it this morning. I haven't had the chance to check—with Leo and everything.'

Mrs Moresby glanced at the bottle. 'Not to worry. She can take one when she's feeling a little less queasy. But we do need to get your brother sorted out. Have you got any medicine in the house?'

Ruby shook her head. 'We just searched. We can't find any.'

Mrs Moresby asked for paper and a pen and scribbled down the name of a medicine. 'They know you down at the pharmacy, don't they?'

Ruby nodded.

'Pop down as quick as you can, and give them this. She handed the note over to Ruby along with some money. Ruby hesitated. 'No arguing,' said Mrs Moresby as if reading her mind. 'And take Mister P with you. It'll give us a bit more space around here.'

Ruby was glad to get out of the flat and into

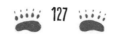

the fresh air. She and Mister P raced all the way to the pharmacy. Luckily Mister P stuck his nose round the door, but decided it wasn't his kind of shop, which made life easier for Ruby.

Then they rushed home again, Ruby clutching the bag with the medicine. As they got to the main entrance to her block, the postman had just arrived. Ruby hesitated for a moment, catching her breath. 'Got anything for 22c?' she asked. Maybe, just maybe, Dad would have remembered to send her a card.

The postman eyed Mister P nervously. 'What's he doing here? Is he safe?'

'Oh yes,' said Ruby. 'He's fine.'

The postman frowned and flicked through his pile of letters very quickly.

'No, sorry. Nothing today.'

The words hit home hard. Nothing today.

Mister P pushed his nose in the direction of the letters as if he wanted to check for himself.

'Get off me,' shouted the postman.

Mister P lifted his head and held out a paw as if trying to shake hands.

The postman screamed, dropped all the letters onto the floor, and RAN.

Mister P stared down at his paw and then looked at Ruby.

'Don't worry,' said Ruby. 'You didn't do anything wrong. You were only trying to help.' She scratched Mister P behind the ears. 'Honestly, some people!'

They returned to the flat to find Mum and Mrs Moresby sitting side by side, drinking tea, and having a quiet chat. They looked so comfortable that Ruby didn't want to interrupt the conversation. She handed over the medicine and she and Mister P went out to their usual spot on the balcony.

'I hope Mum likes Mrs Moresby,' she said. 'It would be nice for her to have a friend to talk to.'

She looked up at the sky and sighed. No letters. No presents.

Happy birthday to me, happy birthday to me . . .

she sang quietly.

Mister P pressed his cold black nose against hers and at that moment, Ruby couldn't think of a nicer present in the whole world.

Dear Dad

I didn't have a great birthday if I'm honest. Leo was ill and none of us knew what to do. Luckily our neighbour, Mrs Moresby, used to be a nurse before she retired (I found that out today by the way) so she came and helped. Leo is much better now in case you are wondering.

Mum hasn't been good either, but Mrs Moresby says it might take longer for her to get better. She says Mum is very lucky to have a daughter like me to look after her and that it isn't my fault when Mum feels bad. I like Mrs Moresby even though she is quite old. She says she would be happy to come and help me out sometimes, but I'm not sure. I don't want to put her to any trouble. She says it's good for her to be busy because it gets a bit lonely when you get older. She doesn't want paying. What do you think?

The good news is that we have managed to give her back almost all of what we owe her for the fish fingers. Mister P did a great job busking at the shopping centre. You should have seen him! Mrs

Moresby says on no account are we to go busking again because we might be arrested and she doesn't want to have to rescue me and Mister P from the police station. She thought that was very funny and laughed a lot when she said it. She also says that it isn't really good for bears to dance in public, but I told her I never MADE Mister P do anything, it was him that wouldn't stop, so she said perhaps that wasn't so bad.

I went to your favourite skateboard shop. Do you remember you promised to give me a skateboard for my birthday one day? I didn't get ANY presents this year (except a polar bear kiss from Mister P). Just saying.

I still miss you and so do Mum and Leo.

Love Ruby

CHAPTER 12

DOUBT AND TRUST

Ruby chewed at her nails. School. There'd be
questions today. There were always questions
when she'd been off. She carefully picked long
strands of polar bear hair off her school uniform
and rolled them into a little ball in her pocket.
It hardly seemed worth going back, not just
for Friday, but she'd promised Mrs Moresby
that she'd go to school if Mrs Moresby
promised not to tell anyone about things at
home. Ruby checked the time on her phone.
She was already late.

'Are you sure you're going to be OK?' she asked Mrs Moresby for about the fiftieth time.

'Go on with you,' said Mrs Moresby. 'We'll be fine. I'll take care of everything.'

'And you'll do it all just like I told you.'

'You're the boss, Ruby,' Mrs Moresby replied. 'I've written everything down, and I've got Mister P to keep an eye on me.'

Ruby wished she could take Mister P to school. She was sure things would be easier at school if Mister P was there.

She arrived and was stopped at reception by the school secretary.

'Could you wait here please, Ruby. The Head wants to see you.'

'But I'm already late,' said Ruby.

The secretary gave her a look and Ruby sighed and sat down.

Ruby knew Mr Bayford quite well on account of spending a lot of time in his office. Mr Bayford wasn't the kind of head teacher who just told you off. He was always really nice and tried to make you talk about things that you did NOT want to talk about . . . like home and parents and that kind of thing. She knew what people said about her behind her back. She was naughty and aggressive; she should learn how to behave or be excluded from school. She didn't need Mr Bayford to explain all this to her again. Maybe Kelly's parents had made an official complaint. She fiddled with the polar bear fur in her pocket.

The door opened and Mr Bayford called her in. He smiled. 'Hello Ruby. Sorry to hold you up, but I thought we should have a little chat.'

Uh-oh, here goes, thought Ruby.

'You've been absent for the last few days

because you have been unwell. Is that right?'
Ruby nodded.

'Are you sure about that, Ruby?'

'Yes! You can call my mum if you don't
believe me.'

'The thing is, I've tried doing that,' said Mr
Bayford, 'But she never answers the phone, does
she? Because she's always too busy at work or
looking after your little brother—or that's what
you told me last time.'

Ruby shrugged. She hadn't bothered to
charge Mum's phone since she'd been at home.
It was the best way of making sure Mr Bayford
could never speak to Mum.

'You see,' Mr Bayford swung his chair to
the left and right and then leant forward on his
desk, 'I've had reports that you've been seen
in Highcross shopping centre with a . . .' Mr
Bayford squinted at his notes, '. . . with a polar
bear.' He chuckled as he said it and his eyebrows
wiggled.

Ruby's
heart
fell. Who could have seen her?

'Of course, that sounds a little far-fetched,'
Mr Bayford continued. 'Except Lucas Pottinger
says his dad was nearly attacked by a polar bear
when he was on his post round yesterday—near
your address.' Mr Bayford raised his eyebrows
and waited.

'Mister P never attacked Lucas's dad. Lucas is
making that up.'

'Mister P? And who is Mister P?'

Now Ruby had landed herself in it. 'No one,'
she said. 'Nothing.'

'You just said that Mister P never attacked Lucas's dad. I want you to tell me who this Mister P is.' The Head's eyebrows went up even further. In Ruby's opinion, Mr Bayford had very overactive eyebrows.

'He's a polar bear,' said Ruby, sighing. 'He followed me home from the park not long ago and now he's moved in with us. I have to look after him 24/7. That's why I had to stay at home.'

'So what were you doing at Highcross then?'

Ruby shrugged. 'Giving him some exercise,' she said. 'Polar bears aren't used to being cooped up.'

'Oh, I see!' Mr Bayford clapped his hands together. 'Well I am going to give you ten out of ten for imagination. I've never had a polar bear used as an excuse for deliberately missing school before. I suppose you and Lucas cooked up this little story between you. But do you know, Ruby, sometimes telling the truth is far easier.'

Ruby couldn't blame Mr Bayford for not believing her, but what else could she say? She pulled the ball of polar bear fur out of her pocket and held it out. Mr Bayford took it and examined it closely.

'A ball of fur doesn't make a polar bear, Ruby.'

'I'm not lying, Mr Bayford,' said Ruby. 'And I wasn't *deliberately* missing school.'

'All right. I will give your Mum one last try. I suppose she can confirm whether or not this polar bear exists?'

'Oh yes,' said Ruby. 'He's there with her now.'

Mr Bayford shook his head and punched the numbers into his telephone. The phone rang once, twice, three times.

'Hello?' Ruby heard a voice on the end of the line, a voice that sounded a lot like Mrs Moresby's.

* * *

Half an hour later, Mr Bayford opened the door of his office for Mrs Moresby. When he saw the polar bear he fainted flat out

on the floor. Dealing with polar bears obviously wasn't part of a teacher's training.

Mrs Moresby activated her nursing skills once again as she put Mr Bayford in the recovery position and waited for him to come round. Ruby fetched him a drink of water and he said he would like to speak to Mrs Moresby and Mister P alone. And THAT was the bit that Ruby was worried about, because what would

he talk to Mrs Moresby about and what would she say? Ruby was sent back to class, but she couldn't concentrate at all. And she could hear people whispering.

Finally, she was summoned back to the Head's office. She couldn't help noticing that he still looked a little pale.

'I am afraid I had to send Mrs Moresby and Mister P home. Health and safety. No polar bears allowed on school premises.'

'I was telling the truth, though,' said Ruby.

Mr Bayford looked Ruby straight in the eye. 'Mrs Moresby has explained that you have a lot of responsibility at the moment and that caring for a polar bear is very demanding and that some allowances should be made at school. So I think we should discuss what we can do to help you. There are other students at school in a similar position.'

Ruby laughed. 'You're not telling me there are other kids trying to look after a polar bear?

I mean how many polar bears have moved in round here?'

'Well no, I don't think anyone else has a bear to look after. But there are children who help care for others at home—family members, that kind of thing—which is probably quite similar.'

'Maybe,' Ruby shrugged. She still wasn't comfortable with this conversation.

'Do you know Marek Sekula in Mr Cheriton's class?' Ruby shook her head. She'd seen Marek around, but she didn't know him. 'Well, he helps take care of his dad. And there are one or two others. It's easier if we know about these things because then we can inform your teachers and make sure you don't get too behind with your work. There are different organizations which can help too.'

Mr Bayford opened his drawer and took out a leaflet. He handed it to Ruby. She glanced at the front. It said something about young carers. She fingered it for a few moments then handed it back. 'They probably don't help with polar bears,' she said.

'Maybe not,' said Mr Bayford. 'But hold onto it anyway.'

Ruby tucked it in her pocket.

'I've been having a think, and I wondered if it might be a good idea for you to move out of Miss Dennis's class and make a new start in Mr Cheriton's room. He's used to working with

Marek and it would give you and Marek the chance to get to know each other.'

Ruby thought about this for a moment. She wasn't that bothered about getting to know Marek, but she'd do anything to get away from Lucas and Kelly.

'Thanks, Mr Bayford,' she said. 'That would be good.'

Mr Bayford made a note on his computer.

'Can I trust you to tell me the truth from now on?' he added.

'I always tell the truth,' said Ruby, crossing her fingers behind her back. 'But I'd rather you didn't mention the polar bear to too many people. He's got used to me looking after him and he wouldn't like it at all if someone came to take him away.'

Mr Bayford nodded and typed another note.

Ruby decided discussing polar bears was certainly a good deal easier than discussing parents.

CHAPTER 13

SPARKLES
AND SURPRISES

Ruby walked fast all the way home. She wanted
to say a hundred thank yous to Mrs Moresby
for not spilling the beans about Mum. And she
wanted to thank Mister P for being a real life
polar bear—even if he did make Mr Bayford
faint.

She let herself into the flat quietly. It was so
quiet, she wondered if anyone was there. She
closed the door and turned around. She had to
squeeze her eyes shut and then open them again
to make sure she wasn't dreaming.

Tied to the back of a chair was a **balloon** with '11' on it. And on the table there was a **cake** with candles and two, large, lumpy-bumpy **presents**. Ruby dropped her school bag on the floor.

SURPRISE!

Mum cried, jumping out from behind a chair. Mrs Moresby came out from behind Ruby's bedoom door with Leo tucked comfortably on her hip, and Mister P burst in from the balcony with a huge grin on his furry face.

'Happy birthday,' said Mum. 'I know we're a day late, but I hope you don't mind.'

Ruby did not mind—not one bit. She was so happy she could have cried.

'I'm sorry,' said Mum. 'You know I would never forget your birthday on purpose. It was only when I was talking to Mrs Moresby today . . . anyway, we hope you like your presents.'

Ruby was so excited she was almost shaking. 'Can I open them?'

Ruby opened the card first. She'd always been told that was the polite thing to do.

> To Ruby
> HAPPY BIRTHDAY
> Love Mum, Leo, and Mister P

She smiled at the three of them then started on the present. First she undid the ribbon and her heart was thump-thump-thumping as she ripped off the paper. She knew what it was. She could feel the shape of it, the weight of it.

The paper fell to the floor and Ruby was left holding the best present she had ever been given: A Shiny blue ...

Not quite new ...

Ripping and roaring ...

SKATEBOARD!

Her very own.

'I've fixed it up for you,' said Mum. 'It's one of your dad's old competition boards. I think he'd like you to have it. He did promise after all.'

Ruby hadn't heard Mum mention Dad's name in ages.

'How did you know?' said Ruby. 'I never told you.'

'Dad and I did talk, you know. Once upon a time.'

Ruby looked over every bit of the board. 'You've done a genius job, Mum. Thank you.'

Mum looked at Ruby and smiled. 'No, it's me who needs to thank *you*,' she said, 'For everything that you do every day.'

Ruby had to stare at the ceiling for a good few moments before she could take everything in. She sniffed loudly and Mister P sniffed too. She wiped her eyes with the back of her hand and Mister P and Mum and Mrs Moresby all did the same. Then Mrs Moresby handed over a smaller present. Ruby ripped it open and inside were knee guards, elbow guards, and a helmet. 'They're not quite new, I'm afraid,' said Mrs Moresby. 'But they'll do the trick. And you need to wear them . . . mark my words.'

Ruby didn't know what to say. She hugged Mum and Leo and Mrs Moresby. And then she turned to Mister P and gave him a high five.

Mum lit the sparkler candles and they fizzed and twinkled just like Ruby fizzed and twinkled inside.

Maybe wishes *did* come true. Even if they were a bit late!

CHAPTER 14

CRASHING AND SMASHING

Ruby decided to wake Mister P up at the crack of dawn to go with her to the park. She wanted to try out her new board without anyone around to see her making a fool of herself. She wouldn't dare go by herself at that time of day, but she felt safe with a polar bear by her side—he'd look after her.

Ruby had always imagined herself as an ace skateboarder, but now it struck her that having a skateboard was one thing, learning to ride it was another—and now she wished more than ever that Dad was here to teach her. Still, she'd read the magazines, so she should be fine. It couldn't be that hard, could it?

She had to start on the flat. That much, at least, she'd worked out. She strapped on her protective gear, clipped on her helmet, and placed her skateboard on the path. Mister P looked on with interest. She tried to remember everything she'd watched her Dad do, but now that the board was in front of her, nothing seemed to work quite as she expected.

She put one foot on the deck and pushed
the board backwards and forwards a few times,
trying to get a feel for it. This was nowhere
near as simple as it looked. She pushed off and
tried to balance, but she'd only gone a couple of
metres before she wobbled, lost her balance, and
jumped off.

Mister P scrunched up his nose—he didn't
look too impressed. Ruby scowled at him. The
second try, she really bailed and smacked
hard onto the tarmac. She rolled onto the grass
and lay on her back, holding her leg, screwing
up her face against the pain. 'Ow, ow, ow,'
she muttered through gritted teeth.

Mister P put his paw over his eyes and sat
down next to her.

'I'm fine,' she said, annoyed. 'It doesn't hurt
that much.'

She tried a third, a fourth, a fifth, and a sixth time. A seventh, eighth, ninth, and tenth! Then she kicked the skateboard out of the way and flopped onto the grass. She'd known it would be hard, but it wasn't supposed to be this hard.

Mister P nudged Ruby with his nose, trying to get her to stand up. She ignored him. He tried again and put one hairy paw on her skateboard to hold it steady. Ruby climbed back on.

'I don't really need your help,' she said, as she clung on to a handful of his fur to keep her balance as he trotted along beside her. 'I can do this by myself, you know.'

Mister P stuck his nose in the air and kept trotting.

Ruby felt the breeze on her face and heard the rolling of the wheels on the path. Gradually she started to get a feel for the deck beneath her feet and loosened her grip on Mister P's fur. So this is what it felt like! She laughed as the ground raced beneath her wheels and soon she was hurtling out of control towards the skatepark with Mister P racing along behind until suddenly . . .

Aaaahhhh!

Mister P grabbed the back of Ruby's dungarees in his mouth and lifted her off the board just as the board smacked straight into the wall surrounding the skatepark. The board

flipped in the air and fell to the ground. Ruby was left dangling from Mister P's teeth.

'What are you doing?' she shrieked. 'I could've stopped. I know what I'm doing!'

From just beyond the wall came the sound of someone laughing. Then a head popped up with a huge grin. 'That's the coolest skateboard trick I've ever seen. What d'you call that one? The polar bear flip?'

Ruby blushed like a tomato and wished Mister P would put her down. The boy came out through the gate, picked up Ruby's skateboard, and carried it to her.

'Nice bear,' he said. 'Is he yours?'

'Nope,' said Ruby, scowling at Mister P.

Mister P opened his jaw and let Ruby drop with a **thump** on the ground. Ruby stood up, brushed herself down, and narrowed her eyes at the polar bear.

'I'm Connor, by the way,' said the boy.

'Ruby,' said Ruby, still blushing.

'And this is . . .?' Connor nodded towards the bear.

'THIS,' said Ruby with her hands on her hips, 'THIS is Mister P.' She'd be having words with the polar bear later.

Connor put up his hand and Mister P gave him a high five. 'Smart bear,' he said. 'Is he a skater too?'

Ruby laughed. 'The bear? No way.'

Connor turned over Ruby's board and examined it carefully. 'This is a great board.' He put the board down then flipped it into his hand. 'Where did you get it from?'

'It was my dad's. Mum fixed it up for me.'

'That's awesome. Well . . . I presume you didn't get up this early just to chat. Shall we go and catch some air?'

Ruby wished she could hide and shuffled closer to Mister P. She tried to think of some good excuse why air was something she wouldn't be catching—not any time soon, at least.

'Everything OK?' asked Connor.

'Yeah. It's just that I can't do any tricks yet. In fact I can't really skateboard at all!'

There. She'd said it. She waited for Connor to walk away. He wouldn't stick around now he knew she wasn't a skater.

'That's insane!' said Connor. 'And with a board like this! Well we all have to start somewhere. I'll help you, if you like?'

'No—it's all right.' Ruby was always suspicious of anyone who was too nice to her. And she certainly didn't expect the coolest rider in the whole skatepark to help a complete beginner.

Mister P put his paw flat on her back and pushed her forwards. She glared at him.

'Come on,' said Connor. 'I can teach you how to stop, at least . . . and I promise I won't use my teeth!'

Now it was Ruby's turn to laugh.

He showed Ruby how to balance her weight on the board. 'Perseverance, determination, guts, and friends . . . that's all it takes to become a skater,' he said. 'Always remember that, because you'll take a few knocks along the way. Now concentrate so you can get some of the basics down before the rest of the gang arrives.'

The rest of the gang? But there was no time to worry about who else might turn up. She was too busy copying everything Connor showed her. For the next hour, Connor did his best to get Ruby going. Mister P watched carefully, turning his head this way and that, blinking as he took in all the information.

Ruby couldn't believe she was so useless. She was desperate to impress Connor, but it just wasn't happening. She pushed off again and—

CRASH!

She attemtped to stop by tipping the back of the board onto the ground and—

CRASH

She tried making her board do little turns and—

CRASH

She took off her helmet and wiped her forehead with the back of her hand.

'I'm never going to be any good,' she wailed.

'You're trying too hard,' replied Connor, smiling. 'It's like anything new—it takes time to get used to it.'

Time was something Ruby didn't have. She checked her watch and her hand flew to her mouth. She'd been concentrating so hard that she'd forgotten about getting home. Mum might need her and Leo would want his breakfast.

She turned to Connor. 'I have to go,' she said.

'You've got to be kidding me. All the others are about to arrive. It's the weekend—this is when the fun starts.'

Your fun, not mine, thought Ruby.

Connor skated backwards and forwards a few times, showing off a few moves. 'You shouldn't give up so quickly,' he said.

'I'm NOT giving up,' said Ruby angrily.

'Prove it.' He gave her a challenging smile.

Ruby's shoulders drooped. If only Connor knew—she'd give anything to spend the day hanging out with the other skaters at the park, but she couldn't. She had other priorities, other responsibilities. She'd have to find her moments and practise when she could.

'Sorry,' she said. She felt the anger start to bubble up, but she bit it back. 'I could try and come back tomorrow.'

Connor saluted her. 'Good. I'll be here.' Then he looked at Mister P.

'Get yourself a board, mate, then you can join in too.'

CHAPTER 15
QUITTERS
AND SURVIVORS

Ruby held on to Mister P's fur and skated along beside him all the way along the path to the road. 'You really know how to make a kid look cool,' she said, sarcastically. 'Have you got any idea how embarrassed I felt back there dangling out of your mouth.'

Mister P grinned and ran a bit faster.

'I might have made a friend, if it hadn't been for you.' She gave Mister P's fur and tug and he put the brakes on so hard, he nearly tipped Ruby off the front of the board.

'OK, OK, well maybe you did help a bit. But the thing is, Mister P, people like Connor will look at me and all he'll see is someone who quits. There are times when I'd love to give up doing the hard stuff like looking after Mum and Leo and getting through a day at school. But I DON'T. And then when I'm doing something I really want to do, like this morning, I have to leave just as the fun is starting and it's not fair.'

They walked on.

Perseverance, guts, determination, and friends.

For Connor, that's what it took to be a skateboarder. For Ruby, it was what she needed to survive.

* * *

'Where have you been, Ruby?' Mum was standing at the door with Leo. 'You've been gone for hours. I've been worried sick.'

'I only went to the park. I wanted to try out my board.'

Mum was angry. 'I don't like you going to the park by yourself early in the morning. You never know who might be about. Anything could happen. I would have come with you.'

'But you were asleep,' Ruby repled. 'And I wasn't by myself—I had Mister P with me.'

Mum looked hurt. 'Mister P this, Mister P that,' she muttered. She slumped down in the arm-chair and switched on the TV, turning up the volume and staring at the screen as if it was the most interesting programme she'd ever seen—which it wasn't.

Ruby was confused. Mum never moaned about her going to the park, and Mum and Mister P seemed to get on very well these days.

Mister P put his head on the arm of Mum's chair and the TV screen went blank.

'Who did that?' said Mum looking around and then directly at the polar bear. 'Shift your head, Mister P, you're on the remote.'

Mister P closed his eyes tight and held his head firm as Mum tried to wrestle the remote from under Mister P's chin. He did not seem to be in a helpful sort of mood. In the end Mum gave up

and the silence in the room stretched and stretched. Mum seemed unwilling to meet Ruby's eye and Ruby wondered what was going on.

'I found your letters,' Mum said, finally. 'The ones you write to Dad.'

Ruby's mouth went dry and she closed her eyes. No wonder Mum was upset. No one was supposed to read those letters—not even Dad—not really.

'They don't mean anything,' said Ruby. 'I've never sent them.'

'Of course they mean something,' Mum said. 'But you could have talked to me, you know, and if you wanted to contact your dad you should have asked me.'

Ruby didn't know what to say. She always tried to avoid mentioning Dad because she was too scared about making Mum even sadder.

'Do you know where he is?' Ruby asked. 'Dad, I mean.' It felt odd saying the word in front of Mum.

Mum shrugged. 'Last I heard, he was in America, but who knows if he's still there.'

Ruby thought about this for a while. 'Would you get better if Dad came back?'

Mum smiled. 'I miss him, Ruby, just like you. But Dad was never one to be tied down.' She shrugged. 'So there we go.'

'So what you're saying,' said Ruby, 'is that when you had us kids, Dad left.'

'No—no! Dad loved you very much Ruby. But it wasn't easy living with me. Not after I got sick.'

'So you got sick and he quit. That's not fair is it? Not on you. Not on any of us.'

Mum thought for a moment. 'I don't think it is as simple as that. He did try to help. But . . . oh it's all too complicated. Skateboarding was his life and . . . well, he didn't seem to be able to do both. He just wasn't that kind of person.' Mum blew a wisp of hair off her face. 'Sometimes I think it's easier having him out of the way.'

Ruby wrapped her arms across her front and tried to work out exactly what Mum was saying. She'd always thought of herself as like her dad, but now she realized that she wasn't really like him at all. She'd never give up on Mum and Leo. **It wasn't about being tied down, it was about stepping up.**

She'd prove that she could take care of Mum and be a good skateboarder and maybe help Mum get better too. Suddenly Ruby felt much stronger. She gave Mum a hug.

'I've got a job for you,' said Ruby. 'And you're not allowed to say no.'

Mum looked at her.

'Mister P needs a skateboard.'

Mum pressed her lips together and her cheeks dimpled. Then she started to laugh. And before long Ruby and Leo were laughing too and poor Mister P seemed to have absolutely no idea what was going on.

'You are kidding, right?' said Mum once she could speak. 'Mister P? Skateboarding?'

'Maybe,' said Ruby. 'We could give it a try, at least.'

'Why not,' said Mum. 'Why not! I'll give it some thought. It won't be easy.'

Ruby smiled quietly to herself. Nothing in life was easy. But that wasn't going to stop her.

CHAPTER 16
RUST AND DUST

Mum turned the key in the padlock to her workshop and the doors squeaked on their hinges as she pulled them open. She flicked the switch and the dark space burst into life. Ruby breathed in the familiar smell of oil and paint. She used to enjoy coming here and watching Mum work. Cars arrived at the workshop looking a complete wreck and left again looking good as new.

'I forgot to tell you,' said Ruby, 'Mr Jay asked if you could fix up his motor. He had an

accident at the traffic lights.'
Ruby folded her arms and
looked pointedly at Mister P,
but he was too busy
sniffing around to notice.

Mum swept back her hair
and put it into a pony tail
then ran her fingers along
the dusty work surface. 'I
suppose it's about time I
cranked this place back into
action,' she said. 'Perhaps I
should *think* about getting
back to work.'

Ruby had heard this all
before. Mum didn't need
to *think* about getting back
to work, she just needed to
do it. Getting her down to
the workshop felt like the
first step.

Mum levered the top off a rusty pot of paint, stuck her nose in, and chucked the whole lot into the bin. Then she squatted down and started pulling stuff out from under benches. 'I've got a pile of old skateboards here somewhere,' she said. 'I'm sure I didn't throw them out.' She hauled out a board with no wheels, then another that didn't look too bad.

'We'll need to spread his weight,' she said. 'One board for each paw.' She found six boards and chose the best four. 'They'll need to be roughly the same size and set-up.'

Ruby loved the energy that came into Mum's face when she got stuck into a project. She watched as Mum

measured and drilled and fixed.

Leo sat happily in his pushchair, enjoying the sights and sounds.

Mister P was sniffing around at the back of the workshop, carefully checking the corners.

'Looking for spiders?' said Mum, glancing up. 'There'll be plenty of them.'

Mister P spun around and scooted towards the workshop doors, swiping at his nose with his front paw.

'I think he just found one,' said Ruby, giggling. She joined him in the sunlight and helped him wipe cobweb off his nose. 'You're not scared of spiders are you, Mister P? A brave bear like you who flies in hot-air balloons?'

Ruby looked at the sky. A plane soared high above them leaving a white trail against the blue. Ruby wondered where it was going.

'It'd be brilliant to be able to fly,' she said. 'Even if it was only in an aeroplane.'

Mister P looked up, gazing at the plane until it was out of sight.

'Perhaps we could both fly off together on our skateboards,' said Ruby, giggling. 'Imagine what fun that would be!'

Mum tinkered for a few more minutes and

then downed tools and called Mister P back into her workshop. 'OK,' she said. 'Here goes.' One by one, Mum strapped each of Mister P's paws to a board. Mister P slid one leg backwards and forwards, and then another. Ruby gave him a

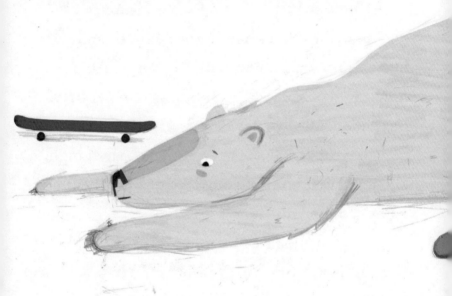

gentle push towards the doors. Mister P's eyes got wider and wider as he rolled across the floor, his four legs getting wider and wider apart. He scrabbled like crazy to try to get some control, but it was too late . . .

SPLAT!

Mister P landed flat on his stomach, legs splayed in four directions like a furry star that had fallen to earth.

'Hmmm,' said Ruby, trying hard not to laugh. 'Maybe a bit more practice is required.'

'Something tells me this bear isn't going to be airborne for quite a while,' said Mum. 'At this rate we're going to be struggling to get him off the ground at all.'

In the end, they had to take off all four boards to allow poor Mister P to scramble back to his feet. He kicked the skateboards out of the way in disgust and walked outside.

'Perseverance,' whispered Ruby, picking up one of the boards and swinging it in front of Mister P's eyes. 'Guts and determination.'

Mister P curled his lip and growled.

'You'll get the hang of it.'

Mister P stuck his nose in the air and wandered off down the street.

Dear Dad

I've had the best weekend ever. I now have my very own skateboard. Mum gave it to me for my birthday. She fixed up one of your old ones and it's brilliant. Yesterday I met a boy called Connor at the skatepark and he's giving me some tips. He can already do a Frontside 180 and he's not that much older than me.

Mum's sorted out Mister P too and he came with me this morning with his new boards. If you think it is hard to learn to skateboard on ONE board, you should try FOUR. Talk about mega-splats! Poor Mister P!

Ruby chewed the end of her pencil and giggled as she thought of Mister P wibbling and wobbling his way through the park, lifting first one leg and then another as he tried to keep his balance. It had been fun having Mister P alongside her. She lost count of how many spectacular crashes he'd had, but each time he just got up, shook himself, and started again. He was so bad he made Ruby look pretty professional.

I met a few other people at the ramp this morning. One is in my new class. His name is Dale and he is OK. Did I tell you I was moving class? I start on Monday.
   Love Ruby

   p.s I have lots of bruises
   p.p.s All my muscles are sore
   p.p.p.s Mister P's muscles are even sorer!

Ruby put her letter in an envelope, but she didn't bother to hide it. She didn't mind if Mum saw it.

CHAPTER 17

DEVELOPMENTS AND DISCOVERIES

A whole week at school—a whole happy-most-of-the-time week.

Her new class was loads better. It felt like a brand new start from the minute she walked in. She was sitting next to Dale and he'd told all the others she was OK. In fact she was so OK she hadn't got angry once—which meant no desk in the corridor and no trips to see Mr Bayford.

She wasn't stupid enough to think that everything was going to be great like this forever, but things had certainly improved. It was good having Mrs Moresby popping in and out to check on things at the flat and she and Mum were becoming good friends. Being in Mr Cheriton's class really helped too. He checked in with her and Marek every morning to see how things were going. Marek always had the same reply, 'You know—up and down.' And the thing was, Ruby did know. And somehow that made things easier for both of them.

She'd managed to get out on her board a couple of times after school with Dale. Mister P had chosen to stay at the flat, but Dale said that was quite likely because he was too exhausted to join them.

'How come you've got the inside info on Mister P?' asked Ruby, feeling a sudden twinge of jealousy.

'Connor says Mister P has been down at the park practising all day while we're at school,' said Dale. 'Apparently he's one **very determined bear.**'

Ruby couldn't help grinning. She'd experienced Mister P's determination before, though sometimes she wondered if he wasn't just plain **stubborn**.

'And how would Connor know? Isn't he at school too?'

'His nan told him,' Dale replied. 'According to Connor, his nan spends a lot of time hanging out with Mister P.'

Ruby's jaw dropped. Of course. OF COURSE! How had she not realized before? Mrs Moresby must be Connor's nan. She thought of the picture in Mrs Moresby's flat, the one of the boy skateboarding, and she laughed out loud.

'What's so funny?' said Dale.

'Oh, nothing,' said Ruby. 'Do you know Connor's nan?'

'He talks about her, but I've never met her.' said Dale. 'I suppose you must know her though if she's so friendly with your polar bear.'

'Yeah, I do,' said Ruby, 'She's a neighbour. But I hadn't realized 'til now that she belonged to Connor!'

Dale and Ruby laughed and carried on walking. 'Is it weird living with a polar bear?' he asked as they reached Mr Jay's.

Ruby shrugged. 'It was hard at first, but you get used to it after a while. It's certainly changed my life quite a lot. I mean you can't exactly ignore it when you have a polar bear living in your flat.'

'I wish I had one in mine!' said Dale grinning. 'He'd sort out my big sister in no time. Could I rent him or something?'

'Maybe . . . one day. I'm planning on sending him round to Lucas and Kelly first. They could learn one or two things about being nice from Mister P, that's for sure.'

Dale gave her the thumbs up. 'OK, Lucas, Kelly, and then me. It's a deal. See you tomorrow.'

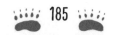

Dale peeled off towards his own home, raising a hand in farewell.

Ruby watched him go and thought about Mister P. Things really had changed since he arrived. For the better.

* * *

That night Ruby didn't feel tired. She was excited about the weekend and getting down to the ramp tomorrow. There was a competition on and she was going to go and watch with Mum and Leo.

But there was something else in the air that was making her restless and she couldn't put her finger on what it was. It wasn't just the excitement. It was a kind of worried feeling and she didn't like it. Mister P seemed restless too. Mind you, she couldn't blame him—it was hot and sticky and the worst kind of night to be a polar bear.

She looked at her watch. Mr Jay's didn't close until ten o'clock and it was only nine now. She'd go and get them both a nice treat. She thought they deserved it after such a good week.

'I told Mum about your car,' said Ruby as she handed a large tub of chocolate ice cream over the counter to Mr Jay.

'I know,' said Mr Jay. 'I took it to her workshop yesterday. She told me she's going to start on it next week.'

Ruby smiled. This was news to her, but it was definitely good news. She paid for the ice cream and ran back to the flat as fast as she could before too much of it melted.

Ruby and Mister P sat at either end of the balcony as the last light from the simmering sun left the sky. The bottom of Ruby's feet rested comfortably against Mister P's paws as she spooned ice cream into her mouth from her bowl and Mister P licked great scoops out of the tub.

'I miss you when I'm at school,' she said. 'But I take a little bit of you in my pocket, you know?' She pulled out the ball of polar bear fur.

Mister P's nose twitched.

'I hear you've been out practising with your skateboards—a lot—that's not very fair on me. I'm not sure you should be out without me around. I hope you haven't been causing trouble?'

Mister P sniffed around the empty ice cream tub in the hope of one last drop.

'We'd better get some sleep, I suppose. Early start.'

Mister P didn't seem in any hurry to move. He grumbled and moaned as he clambered onto all fours.

She put her arm around Mister P's neck and they stood together looking up at the stars.

'What do you wish for, Mister P?'

Mister P just kept looking at the sky and Ruby thought she saw a tear glinting in the corner of his eye.

'Don't look so sad, Mister P. It's the skateboard competition tomorrow. It'll be fun.'

Mister P stared up for a moment longer then dropped his head and padded slowly back into the flat.

CHAPTER 18

BEGINNINGS AND ENDINGS

'Where did you get that from?'

Mister P was wearing a brand new skater cap on his furry head. He had his four skateboards lined up by the front door and was plodding around the flat being very busy. First he went to Ruby's bedroom and fetched his suitcase. This seemed a little strange. After all, the competition was only in the park and hardly called for luggage. Next he went to the kitchen where he hooked one claw round the fridge door and flicked it open. He pulled out the last remaining

packet of fish fingers with his teeth and dropped it into the suitcase.

'Picnic lunch?' she said as Mister P closed the lid of the suitcase. 'You do know that's the very last packet of fish fingers left, so don't eat them all at once. I'll have to talk to Mum about getting some more.'

Mister P sat down by the door, one paw resting on his case.

'Chill out, Mister P,' said Ruby. 'We don't need to leave yet.'

But Mister P seemed anything but chilled. He drummed his claws up and down on the lid of his suitcase until the rest of the family were ready to leave. Mum took Leo down in the lift first and then Ruby and Mister P watched the floors light up as it came all the way back to the 22nd floor to pick them up. In they got and Mister P stuck out his claw and pressed the ground floor button. As the lift started to descend, he gave a long sigh. Ruby smiled. 'I suppose you think this is boring now,' she said. The lift juddered to halt just one floor down and the doors opened.

'Good morning,' said Mrs Moresby cheerily. **'Is there room for one more?** I'm heading to the park to watch the skateboarding competition.' She backed her way into the lift and somehow the door slid closed.

'You told me your grandson didn't like you watching him skateboarding.'

'He doesn't . . . but I'm not coming to watch my grandson, I'm coming to watch Mister P.'

Ruby groaned. 'Please don't tell me that Mister P is taking part in the competition?'

'He most certainly is. He's been preparing all week.'

Ruby looked at the massive bear towering over them and she tapped her fingers against her skateboard. She could think of at least a thousand things that could go wrong with a polar bear getting involved in a skateboard competition and she could do without any more unexpected expenses.

Clearly Connor hadn't said anything to his nan about knowing Ruby, so Ruby didn't say anything about knowing Connor. But she was pretty sure that he wasn't going to be thrilled when he saw Ruby turning up at the park with his nan in tow. This morning had

TROUBLE written all over it.

Once they reached the park, Mrs Moresby and Mum helped Mister P with his boards while Ruby put on her gear. Connor was right: Mister P had been practising. In fact he whizzed along the path so fast, Ruby could barely keep up with him. At least it gave her a chance to warn Connor about Mrs Moresby turning up.

The skatepark was busy with lots of people of all ages warming up for the competition. Rails, stairs, ledges, halfpipes, it was all going on today. Connor spotted Ruby and Mister P and skated over.

'How's it going,' he said, giving them both a high five.

'Your nan's on the way. Just so you know.'

Connor grinned and rolled his eyes. 'So you've worked that out then. Seems Mister P is her new best friend.'

'She's cool,' said Ruby. 'You're lucky. I wish I had a nan like her.'

'She's all right,' said Connor, 'Just as long as she doesn't hang out down here all the time watching me.' The three of them looked at the bench where Mum, Leo, and Mrs Moresby were making themselves comfortable to watch what was going on.

'Why didn't you tell me that Mrs Moresby was your nan?' asked Ruby.

Connor looked at the ground and lifted one shoulder very slightly. 'I didn't want you to think I was helping you out just because you knew her.'

'And were you?' said Ruby, suddenly uncomfortable.

'NO!' said Connor. 'I was helping you out because that's what friends do and it because it was funny watching you fall off all the time. Oh, and I liked your bear.'

Ruby scowled and then realized from Connor's huge grin that he was joking. Dale skated over to join them and they all high-fived.

A big bubble of happiness floated up in Ruby's chest.

Friends! At long last she really had friends.

They helped Mister P with his skateboards and the three of them watched him roll into the half-pipe. He cruised backwards and forwards, bending his hairy knees, and shifting his weight to produce his own polar version of the frontside ollie—skating up the vertical, lifting into the air, turning, and coming back down again.

Ruby's eyes widened. 'How's he learnt that so quickly?'

'He's a natural,' said Connor. 'He's got a great sense of balance—maybe it comes from living on the ice or something.'

'Maybe,' said Ruby as she watched skaters spinning out of the way to avoid the massive flying bear. 'Though I'm not sure skateboarding is big in the Arctic.'

'Perhaps Mister P could introduce it. You know, when he goes home,' said Dale.

'Our flat is his home now,' said Ruby. 'He's not going anywhere.'

The announcements began so Ruby left the park and went to take her seat with Mum, Leo, and Mrs Moresby. The competitors stood in groups in their brightly coloured shorts, each one holding their skateboard. There was a short delay as the organizers didn't seem quite certain what to do with a polar bear. But as he'd already attracted a big crowd of admirers, it was decided he should skate last—as the grand finale. In the meantime he was sent to wait with Ruby.

The competition got underway, and Ruby's heart beat faster as she watched the incredible tricks. It reminded her of the buzz of excitement she used to get when watching Dad, but now it was her, here with her friends. The crowd cheered and skaters punched the air as they nailed their tricks. Others didn't do so well and everyone gasped as they bailed and slid down the ramp on their sides. Connor was easily the best, but Dale messed up so badly, he managed to damage his board. Mum said to tell him to bring it to the workshop after school and she'd see what she could do to fix it up. This made Ruby smile. She felt proud to have Mum sitting beside her.

The closer it got to Mister P's turn, the more fidgety he became. Connor, Dale, and some others from the skatepark came and joined Ruby so they could all watch Mister P together. Ruby felt nervous. She hoped Mister P wouldn't make a fool of himself.

'Don't worry,' said Ruby, 'We're all here to cheer you on. You'll be great.'

Mister P turned to Ruby and touched his

nose against hers. She took off his cap and
scratched the fur between his ears, then she
closed her eyes and felt his warm breath
on her face.

'Good luck,' she whispered.
He picked up his suitcase in his teeth.
'Wait,' said Ruby. 'What are you taking that
for?'

Mister P ignored her and walked slowly to the top of the ramp. Maybe his suitcase was like his good luck charm or something. Ruby reached for Mum's hand and held it tight. Mister P positioned his weight over the boards, stared down into the half pipe and then out into the distance. He still had the handle of his suitcase gripped firmly between his teeth. Ruby held her breath.

Mister P took one final look in Ruby's direction and held her eye for a few seconds. Then he dropped in on the left side of the ramp and flew up the vertical on the other side. He lifted high into the air and sailed over the park fence, landing perfectly on his four boards.

And then he kept going . . .
and going . . .
and going.
'Wrong way, Mister P,' shouted
Connor, laughing. 'Come back!'
'What are you doing?' shouted Dale?
'Where are you going?' shouted Mum.

But their shouts got lost in the empty air and slowly they all went silent.

And then Ruby knew . . . or thought she knew . . .

. . . that Mister P had gone . . .

. . . forever.

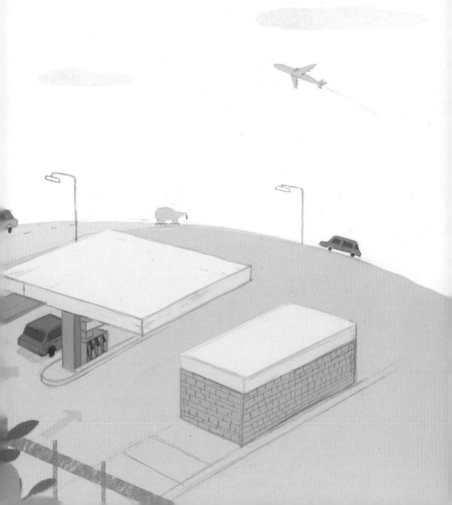

Now everyone was looking at her. Ruby's breath caught and she swallowed down the lump in her throat.

'Well that's one less thing for me to worry about,' she said, picking up his cap and pulling pieces of polar bear fur off it. 'No more embarrassing trips to the supermarket, no more dancing on the streets, no more sharing my room with a smelly mountain of bear hair.' She tried to blink away the tears.

Connor took off his helmet, scratched his head, and frowned. 'No more accidents in the skatepark? No more polar bear tricks?'

'No more fish fingers, at least,' said Mrs Moresby.

Leo started sobbing.

'He'll probably come back,' said Mum.

But Ruby knew. Mister P would not come back. She rolled the polar bear fur into a tiny ball and put it in her pocket.

Dear Dad

How are you? I nailed the 'drop-in' on the ramp today. It was dead cool. You would have been impressed.

Mister P has been gone for three whole months now so I don't think he'll be coming back. I suppose it's good really because we're not supposed to keep animals in the flat and it was quite crowded with him around.

Ruby picked up Mister P's cap and fingered it. It still smelt like polar bear.

Mum says people come and go for different reasons. Some stay when it's good and leave when it's bad. Others stay when it's bad and leave when it's good, because they know you can do all right without them.

If Mister P ever catches up with you on the skateboard circuit, tell him that we're doing all right, but that we miss him very badly. I still have to look after Mum and Leo some of the time, but Mum is back to work most days and now that Mister P has gone, Mrs Moresby helps with Leo instead.

I think I will post you this letter. I wonder if you will get it.

Love Ruby

XOXO

Ruby folded the letter carefully, put it in an envelope, and wrote Dad's address on the front.

CHAPTER 19

SUNSHINE AND CLOUDS

Ruby popped Dad's letter into the postbox and then walked to the park with Leo. She stopped to say hi to Connor and Dale.

'Not skating?' they said.

Ruby shook her head. 'I'm taking Leo to feed the ducks. Mum's not having the best week.'

'Is Nan with her?' asked Connor.

'Yep—she's taken Mum to her appointment at the hospital.'

'Cool,' said Connor. 'We'll come with you to the pond then.'

Dale and Connor put Leo onto a skateboard and held one hand each as they let him roll towards the pond. Ruby followed with the pushchair. There's no way Leo would be waiting until he was eleven to start skating!

'Ack!' called Leo as the ducks gathered close to the edge of the pond. Dale and Connor helped Leo throw bread into the water.

Suddenly the ducks went very still and Ruby frowned. A dark shadow was drifting across the pond towards them, turning the water black.

'Midder P, Midder P!'
Leo shouted, jumping up and
down and pointing at the sky.

Ruby's heart beat a little faster
as she looked up. A huge cloud was
crossing the sky, blotting out the sun.

'No, Leo, not Mister P. Just a cloud.'

'Midder P,' said Leo, his little voice dropping
and his hand falling back to his side. Ruby
wrapped Leo in a massive bear hug.

'He was a star, that bear,' said Connor.

'Some of the time,' said Ruby. And even
though she felt sad, she couldn't help smiling.

SKATING TRICKS

BIG BEAR AIR

Big Air is when you launch off a ramp and gain lots of height, so a Big Bear Air is even more impressive and performed by a Polar Bear!

The **Ollie** trick involves bending your knees, and pressing down on the back of the board with your back foot. The front of the board will lift up and the back will 'pop' off the ground. Then drag your front foot forward to balance the board out whilst off the ground and land. This can be used to jump over or onto objects in the street or skate park.

OLLIE

KICKFLIP

WOW

🐾 The **Kickflip** is a trick to try once you have mastered the Ollie. It's a similar process to the Ollie, but when you pop off the ground, quickly slide your foot to the front of the board, 'kick' out, and flick the edge of your board with your little toe. This will cause your board to 'flip' around. Once the board fully rotates, you should land with your back foot first and knees bent. A little tip to get better at the kickflip is to try and Ollie as high as you can first. This will give you more time off the ground and longer to flip the board around, but it's a difficult trick so be patient!

There are so many cool tricks to learn, such as a 180 No-Comply or a Pop Shove It, or why not make up your own, like Ruby here!

The main thing to remember is to have fun!

MORE
MISTER P
FUN ...

The bear stood like a statue. Inside Arthur's very still body, his ♥ was thumping and inside his very still head his mind was racing. He thought it best to seem friendly so he nodded and smiled at the polar bear. The bear nodded at Arthur and bared its long, sharp teeth.

Arthur was terrified. He tried to think of a plan, but he wasn't very good at plans and he'd never had to make one involving a polar bear before. He decided he needed to catch the bear unawares, dart past him, and run for home. It wasn't much of a plan but it was the best he could come up with. The trouble was, he wasn't exactly sure what made a bear unaware.

Arthur looked at the ground and the bear looked at the ground.

He looked at the sky and the bear looked at the sky.

Hmm, thought Arthur. He covered his eyes with his hands and, when he opened his fingers just enough to peep through, he saw the polar bear had covered its eyes with its paws—and Arthur was pretty certain that you couldn't peep through a paw.

This was Arthur's chance.

He'd run for it while the bear wasn't looking.

He tiptoed past the bear and then sprinted at top speed. He didn't stop to look over his shoulder. He didn't dare listen for the sound of huge paws

thud,
thud,
thudding

behind him.

He ran all the way home, as fast as his legs would carry him, let himself into his house, slammed the door, and flicked the lock on the safety latch. He leant against the door, breathing hard.

'Arthur, is that you?' Dad asked, poking his head round the living room door. 'Where have you been?'

'I ran away,' gasped Arthur, still out of breath. 'For EVER. Not that anyone noticed.'

ABOUT THE AUTHOR

Maria Farrer lives in a house in the middle of a field in Somerset with her husband and her very spoilt dog. She used to live on a small farm in New Zealand with a flock of sheep, a herd of cows, two badly behaved pigs, and a budgie that sat on her head while she wrote. She trained as a speech therapist and teacher and later she completed an MA in Writing for Young people. She loves language and enjoys reading and writing books for children of all ages. She likes to ride her bike to the top of steep hills so she can hurtle back down again as fast as possible. She also loves mountains, snow, and adventure and one day she dreams of going to the Arctic to see polar bears in the wild.

ABOUT THE ILLUSTRATOR

Daniel Rieley is a British freelance illustrator based
in Lisbon. After studying at The Arts Institute
Bournemouth, undertaking an epic backpacking
adventure in Australia, and working for three years in
London, he decided to take off to sunny Portugal. For
the past few years, Daniel has been working on several
illustration projects from advertising, print, and card
design to children's books.

When Daniel is not drawing, you can probably
find him trying to catch waves, taking photos with old
cameras, or playing his newly discovered sport, Padel.

Here are some other stories we think you'll love ...